SUCCESS SECRETS

SUCCESS SECRETS OF BLACK EXECUTIVES

FROM THE EDITORS OF

ISBN 0-935-419-04-7
LIBRARY OF CONGRESS CATALOGING AND CLASSIFICATION
NUMBER 92-076198
© 1992 ELECTRON ACCESS INC.
530 HOWARD STREET
SAN FRANCISCO, CA 94105
FOR ORDERS, (800) 358-5781
BY FAX (415) 777-3191

From The Editors Of ASPIRE

SUCCESS SECRETS OF BLACK EXECUTIVES
©1992 ELECTRON ACCESS INC
SAN FRANCISCO, CA 94105

All rights reserved, domestic and foreign. No part of this book may be reproduced or transmitted in any form or by any means, electronic or mechanical, including photocopy, recording or any information storage and retrieval system, without the written permission of the publisher.

Printed in the United States of America.
Headlines in Helvetica Black
Body type in Trump Medieval

ISBN 0-935-419-04-7
Library of Congress Cataloging in Publication Number 92-076198

Stories appearing in this book originally appeared in the following ELECTRON ACCESS INC. publications: *ASPIRE, Bay Options, Bay Engineer, Bay BusinessWoman and the Black Executive Forum.*

We gratefully acknowledge the support of the participants and speakers in the *Black Executive Forum* series and the following host organizations: Silicon Graphics Inc., California Biotechnology Inc., Grubb & Ellis, Stanford University Graduate School of Business, Katia LaCoste Gallery and Bourbon Street.

SUCCESS SECRETS OF BLACK EXECUTIVES

INTRODUCTION

I was 34 years old before I met an African-American chief financial officer of a publicly---traded corporation.

That says a lot about the nature of racism in America.

During the next several years, I and my fellow writers at ASPIRE Books and Magazines interviewed dozens of African-American chief financial officers, vice presidents of manufacturing, voice mail inventors, scientific workstation designers, missile makers, atomic supersleuths and international sales executives -- both men and women.

Their presence says volumes about the progress of black business executives in spite of the continuing presence of bias throughout the economy.

Most of those volumes had not been committed to paper, meaning that generations following us continue to believe that "blacks can't do..."

Believe us, we do it all.

As you will read.

And we do it with the same flair and grace that marks our success in entertainment and athletics.

As the 21st century approaches, there is a return to the entrepreneural spirit that marked the end of the 19th century.

During that era, many of the oldest African-American businesses were created, on a shoestring, without the benefit of advanced training and strategies.

In the 21st century, the same pressures of increasing discrimination will drive us toward a renewed emphasis on creating our own jobs. This time, we'll be equipped with decades of the best preparation that academic and corporate America could buy, and with international opportunities our ancestors could never have dreamed of.

Success Secrets provides the guidebook for following in the footsteps of those pioneers. We publish these success secrets in the

FROM THE EDITORS OF ASPIRE

hope that today's and tomorrow's business pioneers will become the new heroes of African-American young people in the same way that the Paul Cuffees, Pio Picos, Giles B. Jacksons and C.C. Spauldings of the last century were.

John William Templeton
Executive Editor
ASPIRE Books & Magazines

TABLE OF CONTENTS

Introduction 3
Part One -- The Overlooked Overachievers
Chapter I - The Road to the Top 9
Chapter II-Rules of the Game   15
Part Two -- Success Secrets
Chapter III-Mastery 19
Chapter IV-Indispensibility 25
Chapter V-Networking 27
Chapter VI-International Experience-37
Chapter VII-Creativity 41
Chapter VIII-Risk Taking 45
Chapter IX-Balance and Time Management 47
Chapter X-Targeting a Niche 51
Chapter XI-Keeping Options Open 55
Chapter XII-Innovative Salesmanship 57
Chapter XIII-Enjoyment 61
Chapter XIV-Self-Assessment 64
Chapter XV-Measurability 69
Chapter XVI-Mentoring 71
Chapter XVII-The Corporate Environment 73
Part Three -- The Next Step
Chapter XVIII-Entrepreneurship 81
Chapter IXX-The Stages of Black Business Development 85
Chapter XX-Maggie L. Walker 87
Chapter XXI-C.C. Spaulding 93
Chapter XXII-Moving into the Third Stage 96
Part Four -- The Fourth Stage
Chapter XXIII-The Fourth Stage 105
Chapter IXXV-Fourth Stage Opportunities 110
Chapter XXV-Blueprint for a Fourth Stage Business 138
Chapter XXVI-Overcoming Mental Slavery 148
Appendices   165
African-American Consumer Market

FROM THE EDITORS OF ASPIRE

PART ONE
THE OVERLOOKED OVERACHIEVERS

SUCCESS SECRETS OF BLACK EXECUTIVES

FROM THE EDITORS OF ASPIRE

I
THE ROAD TO THE TOP

"When the right circumstances exist, we can make it. So we have to work on creating the right circumstances."

Dr. Walter Massey, director, National Science Foundation and past chairman of the American Association for the Advancement of Science. Former member of the President's Council of Science Advisors.

By John William Templeton

Dr. Walter Massey is a perfect example of the "overlooked overachievers" who are quietly sweeping through the American economy.

In 1990, a paper was presented at the American Association for the Advancement of Science (AAAS) which purported to debunk differences in intelligence between blacks and whites. This study drew much of the mass media coverage of the event.

Not a single newspaper mentioned the living contradiction at the convention to that hypothesis. The AAAS, the leading association of scientific inquiry, was headed by quantum physicist Dr. Massey, an African-American native of rural Hattiesburg, Miss and graduate of historically-black Morehouse College.

His field of research for the past 30 years has been "many body" theories of quantum liquids and solids. In lay language, he studies particles smaller than atoms to determine the nature of matter.

Most Americans, black or white, would never picture an African-American playing such a critical role in a highly scientific field. The first superstar from Chicago to come to their mind would be Michael Jordan.

However, there are many more Walter Masseys than Michael Jordans. In fact, there are more African-American Ph.d's in physics (300) in the United States than there are African-American players in the National Basketball Association (approximately 235).

SUCCESS SECRETS OF BLACK EXECUTIVES

That statistic flies in the face of conventional wisdom and the image portrayed of African-Americans as a pathological conglomeration of gang members, rappers, welfare mothers, dope dealers and unemployed laborers blithely inseminating teenagers without regard for their ability to provide for their families.

In the most charitable popular analysis, black Americans are seen as a mutated shadow of the dominant European-American culture, frustrated over their inability to master the techniques of th e "mainstream."

This view was prevalent in the early movies of the 20th century, according to historian Daniel Goode.

> "Prejudice against black people appeared almost at the beginning of the film industry...During this period, the common and persistent theme in films dealing with octoroons and mulattoes was the apparent shame and degradation of being identified as nonwhite. The obvious implication exploited here was something innately subhuman in being black. Indeed, the lesson seemed to be, as evidenced in several productions, that for the unfortunate octoroon or mulatto, suicide was the only escape from a world where to be partially black was a worse fate than to be a full-blooded black.[1]

Observers of today's mass media will see the resemblance to that founding vision in the themes of many of today's movies and television shows, even as we near the end of the 20th century.

But nowhere is Ralph Ellison's "Invisible Man" more transparent than on the business pages of America's newspapers, magazines and books. There are very few models of African-American business success, not to mention scientific expertise, in the mass media.

For instance, Massey has managed to avoid media attention despite rising to become director of the National Science Foundation , in charge of the largest federal funding source for civilian science research.

FROM THE EDITORS OF ASPIRE

Before that job, Massey was vice president of research at the prestigious University of Chicago, in charge of the Argonne National Laboratories, home of some of the world's most advanced nuclear research. He sat on the boards of Amoco Corp., First National Bank of Chicago, Motorola, Continental Materials Corp., the Tribune Co., Brown University, the Rand Corp. and was founder of the Chicago High Tech Association.

But Massey is not an aberration. Outside the glare of media scrutiny, black Americans took the ball and ran with the Great Society advances of the 1960s and 1970s. While Jim Brown was paving the way for the O.J. Simpsons, Walter Paytons, Eric Dickersons and Tony Dorsetts that followed into the National Football League, a wave of black Americans followed the blocking of Thurgood Marshall, James Meredith and Martin Luther King Jr. into an unprecedented assault on American institutions of higher learning.

The Los Angeles Times reported in November 1991:

> "Over the last three decades, the number of black Americans officially counted as middle class -- or "affluent" in the language of the Census Bureau -- has grown by almost 400 percent, more rapidly than any other racial category in American society. More than 1 million black households are listed by the Census Bureau as "affluent" with incomes of $50,000 or more, and they are enjoying a middle-class lifestyle that was beyond the reach of their parents and grandparents. The figure, about 14 percent of the nation's black population, is up sharply from 1967, when only 266,000 black households, or 5.8 percent of the total, were considered affluent."[2]

At ASPIRE magazine, we were amazed at the results of a survey of the African-American population in California by the highly-

SUCCESS SECRETS OF BLACK EXECUTIVES

respected research firm of Impact Resources Inc. of Columbus, Ohio.3

The percentage of black civilian employees holding managerial and professional jobs was 27.4 percent. The next ranking category was clerical employees at 14.3 percent, followed by factory workers at 11 percent. Sales workers accounted for nine percent.

A second research project involved locating those households. In conjunction with Consumer Marketing Research of Hoboken, N.J., we performed a cross-tabulation between California driver's license records and households identified as high income. Driver's licenses specify race, making it possible to identify black families with income above $35,000.

That tabulation resulted in a quarter million households in just California. Clearly something was happening that did not fit the headlines.

ASPIRE founder John Templeton got hit squarely in the face with this trend after assuming a position as editor of the *San Jose Business Journal*, the business newspaper serving high-tech Silicon Valley. At the time, he was the first African-American to serve as editor of a local business journal in American history.

Along with his publisher, he hosted a get acquainted breakfast for a dozen top valley executives. Four of the twelve were African-American. It was hard to see who was more surprised -- Templeton -- or the black executives. He had never seen more than one African-American corporate vice president in the same room and they had never seen a black man editing a business newspaper.

A seed was planted among them, that began to grow once the Business Journal was sold to another newspaper chain. Templeton launched his own publication geared to the African-American managerial and professional market.

Over a three-year period, the list of African-American senior corporate executives in the immediate Bay Area grew to more than 200, and very few of them knew each other. A reception led to a series of monthly meetings and an annual ranking.

In the process, some valuable lessons and patterns emerged. We've

FROM THE EDITORS OF ASPIRE

compiled them into a road map that anyone can follow.

FROM THE EDITORS OF ASPIRE

II
THE RULES OF THE ROAD

"In being successful, there are plenty of barriers. The challenge is how to rise above those barriers. You can't get turned off. You never quite know why things are difficult, but I contend that it doesn't really matter."

Kenneth Coleman, senior vice president, Silicon Graphics Inc.
Founder, Peninsula Area Black Personnel Administrators

The most therapeutic part of the Black Executive Forum encounters was for senior executives to find someone with whom they could relate. When we began compiling a Bay Area corporate executive list, none of the executives knew more than three other blacks at a similar level. Most thought they were the only one in the Bay Area.

That meant that they had to internalize much of the frustration and pressure that accompanied their progress. To be an African-American corporate executive in the United States is to bear a double responsibility, to the shareholders and to the race. The latter responsibility comes whether they want it or not.

Dr. Wayne Wormley of Drexel University reports from a longitudinal paired study of 814 black managers and 814 white managers that there are major differences in the treatment and expectations accorded to the two groups. The blacks are less familiar with available training opportunities and less autonomy in their roles. They also received lower performance ratings and were judged less promotable. The black managers were more likely to have unmet expectations from the company.[4]

One of his findings was:

> **"Black managers are rarely viewed as individuals. The entire race or color is viewed as a whole."**

SUCCESS SECRETS OF BLACK EXECUTIVES

The attendees in the Forum had struggled with that feeling for years, but had alternated between feeling overly paranoid and ignoring it.

A common experience was the feeling of never being validated, no matter what their accomplishments. It was earthshaking to hear this among a group that had, for example:

- invented the fastest computer circuit capable of driving a scientific workstation;
- handled the finances for the largest leveraged buyout in American history;
- managed fast-growing startups that were listed among the hottest companies in America.

In the town where Shelby Steele spoke of "the content of one's character," there was no support for the hypothesis of the "color-blind society" among some of the most accomplished African-Americans in American business.

If moving up the corporate ladder means "climbing up the rough side of the mountain," then thousands of black Americans have certainly managed to do it. However, thousands more have crashed and burned on the runways of corporate America unprepared for the insidious ethnocentrism that permeates most corporate environments.

By sharing the strategies that have worked for the "corporate superstars," then those e ratios can be improved.

In Part Two, we outline some of the strategies that have e worked for those have passed through the gauntlet. We add this caveat. Unlike a football game, with a definite goal line, these corporate competitors rarely get a chance to rest on their laurels. Their struggle is a never ending one.

In the three years we've followed this group -- we've noticed the effect of the glass ceiling. Very few have risen from the vice president level to the chief executive's chair.

From The Editors of ASPIRE

PART ONE
A DOZEN SUCCESS SECRETS THAT WORK FOR SUCCESSFUL AFRICAN-AMERICAN EXECUTIVES

- MASTERY
- INDISPENSIBILITY
- NETWORKING
- INTERNATIONAL EXPERIENCE
- CREATIVITY
- RISK TAKING
- ENJOYMENT
- ASSESSMENT
- MENTORS
- MEASURABILITY
- BALANCE
- ORGANIZATION
- PRESENTATION

Success Secrets of Black Executives

FROM THE EDITORS OF ASPIRE

III
MASTERY

"I always asked for the tough job and tried to become an expert at it. When I come out of the military, I decided to go into manufacturing because it's very accountable. To an extent, I controlled my own destiny.

> Joe Booker, Vice President-Manufacturing, Network Computing Devices Inc., Former President, Priam Corp.

Contrary to popular belief, the highest-ranking African-American corporate executives primarily work in direct line-management positions with bottom-line responsibility.

As Booker notes, serving in a measurable role is a good way to avoid the kind of subjective evaluations where insidious racism can creep in and damage one's career.

A good example has been Joe Avery, the grandson of a Florida preacher who decided to go into chemistry after seeing a picture of a lab technician in a magazine.

"So that's what I decided I wanted to be," says Avery. "My grandfather was a minister and he was pushing me to be one, too."

"I was in college studying chemistry before I learned what a lab technician actually did," quips the burly, yet soft-spoken executive. Avery then set his sights a letter higher.

After a stint in the military handling advanced technology, he rose through the ranks at Hewlett-Packard to become a manufacturing manager.

In 1986, Avery was recruited by a headhunter (executive searcher) to take over manufacturing operations for Adept Technologies Inc. in San Jose, California. Adept has developed several product lines of factory robots, vision systems and flexible automation devices.

The technology is at the forefront of American manufacturing competitiveness. Adept's robots work through high torque motors located in the moving joints of the robot, operating through instructions pumped by powerful amplifiers.

"The result is absolute feedback at all times," says Avery. "You always know where the motor is. There are no chains, no gears. It's servo-feedback as opposed to mechanical systems."

For a factory operator, that means the moving parts of the robot will go exactly where the computer signals tell it to, a problem for mechanical systems that work on pulley and gear combinations. "It's a one to one ratio at all times," says Avery. "Because of the powerful amplifiers, there's no time wasted receiving instructions."

The success of the system has propelled Adept to be one of Inc. magazine's highest growth companies, with a large percentage of its systems imported to Europe and Japan. Quality is a key component of that success.

"We have a very low DOA (dead on arrival) rate, which means that the robot does not fail within the initial 60-day period," Avery notes. "We ship no robot without 100 hours of testing."

Avery monitors all factors that impact the production process. He oversees materials, production, engineering, quality assurance and facilities. On a monthly basis, he meets with the company president and fellow vice presidents of marketing, sales and finance to review the master production schedule. "We agree on a schedule over the horizon of a year, focusing on the next quarter," he notes. Robots are shipped within 60 to 90 days of an order.

The manufacturing chief stays competitive by developing manufacturing techniques as new products are designed. "By the time the product completes its trial run, the next run is a manufacturing run."

From his corner office suite, Avery is planning to introduce more automation into his factory. His office is a few feet away from a spotless, smooth-flowing facility in which simplicity is king.

At each station, parts drop easily into the assembly along a conveyor that sweeps around the perimeter at a 45 degree angle. At the end of the line, robot begin their testing.

FROM THE EDITORS OF ASPIRE

From the other direction, the computer-based controller units move toward completion and wind up at the same testing area. Once both controller and robot finish testing, they move out into the shipping area.

Avery wants to begin automation in the test area, so that operator can monitor a number of machine at once an so that testing can go on 24 hours a day.

"You can tell a lot about an organization by looking at its manufacturing process," says Avery. "The combined ills of an organization are reflected in its manufacturing from poor decisions about products, designs or people."

His concerns about manufacturing extend beyond his facility. He reads books like Richard Schomberger's "World Class Manufacturing" and Yasuhiro Monden's "Toyota Production System" as part of his homework regimen. "I usually will take one day of the weekend to just catch up on my reading," Avery says.

"We're in the process of losing our manufacturing capability as a nation," he predicts with an eye at the growing sales of his robots abroad while American firms still grapple with introducing new methods. "There's a lack of investment in manufacturing. You only find isolated pockets like Hewlett Packard and Tandem, that are good breeding grounds for manufacturing managers. In the typical management team, we're not recruiting top folks for manufacturing. They're going into R&D or marketing."

"Very few schools have a good program in manufacturing," he adds. "The average MBA might take one or two courses in production management. So where are we learning it?"

Avery recommends operations as a career choice "because it's measurable and you get the satisfaction of knowing you made something better than anyone in the world."

He takes pride in the use of Adept robots and vision systems in state-of-the-art plants like Next Inc. and Apple Computer's Macintosh factory, both in Fremont, California.

Avery has also known the satisfaction of building a company from the ground up. "I'd like to see us get to the size of Sun Microsystems

($1 billion) in the next few years."

For that far-reaching goal, like many others in his life, one would probably want to put their money on Joe Avery.

He makes things happen.

FROM THE EDITORS OF ASPIRE

IV
INDISPENSIBILITY

"The most important part of any company is the people. I have not a successful company with a bad president."

Damion Wicker, M.D., M.B.A., medical venture capitalist

Ron Williams and a brand new management team had a big mess to clean up at Blue Cross of California, the state's largest health care insurer, in 1988.

He had just taken a start-up outpatient substance abuse company to the stage of attracting outside investment when he was asked to join Blue Cross.

"What attracted me to Blue Cross was that I had never done a turnaround," says Williams.

During his first year as vice president for corporate services, Blue Cross lost $50 million on revenues of $2 billion. For 1989, the company earned $80 million.

Williams was promoted to executive vice president for health products and services with responsibility for the California Care health maintenance organization, optical and dental plans, corporate marketing and the medical department.

The turnaround was painful. "When I came, we literally didn't know how many employees we had. We reduced from 6,500 full time equivalent positions to 3,700 full-time equivalents."

"Interestingly enough, we reduced claim processing time from 17 days to 11 days," noted Williams. "It was three years of driving people crazy through a single-minded focus on process simplification."

The company took a hodge-podge process and turned each product line into a strategic business unit. "One person had accountability for the total process by bringing the functions together into a full service activity. Before that, the flow made absolutely no sense." With that accountability came lots of tough questions. "I call it the difference between show-me management and tell-me management. We made people prove everything."

In addition to process simplification, the insurer has also turned to technology to achieve greater efficiency. "We used to receive 250,000 phone calls per month for pharmacy claims. We switched to a point of service delivery system in which claims are process through bar codes. We can check eligibility and benefits on-line and the claim is filed electronically, so neither the customer, the pharmacist nor us has a paperwork burden because of the prescription."

Williams doesn't feel Blue Cross is out of the woods yet. "We still haven't made back the money we lost yet, and it's a cyclical business --always has been. We just hope we can avoid the depths of the cycle through acyclical revenue sources and profitable growth."

Underwriting income has grown every year for the past three years, meaning the company has been able to accurately predict the rate of growth in health care costs. "But with $2 billion in premium revenue, if we miss it by one percent, that's a $20 million hit in our earnings. If we miss it by three percent, that's $60 million."

As a regulated business, the political environment is important to those projections. Williams took note of a proposal by Speaker Willie Brown to mandate that insurance companies provide health coverage to smaller businesses by creating a reinsurance pool. The legislation is inspired by statistics that 6 million Californians are not covered by health insurance at all. "The hot political issue of the 1990s will be health insurance," predicts Williams.

"We're in the middle, between the doctors and the employers who pay for the coverage. There's a lot of physician bashing, but we don't think they're the problem when you look at the malpractice costs they have and other increased costs."

One cost-containment approach has been preferred provider organizations (PPO). Blue Cross' Prudent Buyer Plan, with 1.3 million members, is the largest insurer PPO in the nation. About

FROM THE EDITORS OF ASPIRE

half the active practicing physicians and 251 hospitals participate by agreeing to charge rates set by Blue Cross in return for getting referrals of Blue Cross patients. Patients are given incentives for using Prudent Buyer providers.

Dr. James Woods, a San Francisco orthopedic surgeon in the audience and president of the local affiliate of the National Medical Association, is one of those member physicians. He notes that minority providers tend to be underrepresented in s such plans and can lose patients because of incentives to use PPOs and IPAs, organizations where doctors are paid a flat fee on a monthly basis for the number of members in a given area.

Williams, who has responsibility for the medical department, agreed to look into that issue.

As one of the three African-American senior executives at Blue Cross, Williams said he is looked to to provide a "sensitivity" to how the company relates to minorities. "The environment is very good because we have succeeded in creating an environment in which achievement is rewarded and we have a workforce that is reflecting of the community."

SUCCESS SECRETS OF BLACK EXECUTIVES

From The Editors of ASPIRE

V
NETWORKING

"When's the last time you've seen a job for a vice president of a corporation advertised in the newspaper?"
Bob Sanders, Alphanumeric Inc. executive search firm

It is not an accident that Silicon Graphics Inc. became the rare American publicly traded company with two African-Americans among its top six executives.

The seeds of that milestone started almost two decades earlier when Ken Coleman, a human resources manager at Hewlett Packard Co. met Howard Smith, an H-P engineering manager.

"I noticed that out of all the people I met and shared information with that Ken and I always shared information that was critical to each other's career," Smith recalls.

Smith described the elements of effective networking for an audience of two dozen senior executives from Bay Area corporations and a dozen African-American managers from Silicon Graphics Inc., the host for the event. Smith and Coleman were both then senior vice presidents at SGI, a $200 million three-dimensional graphic workstation manufacturer.

He laid out a simple test on networking. "If you find that you're routinely finding out about things through press releases and management announcements and go into meetings where everyone know about the change except you, then you need to really expand your network," Smith says.

The two-way flow of timely information is critical to executive success. Smith recalls that he probably would have left H-P prematurely after not getting a promotion he thought he deserved. However, a friend walked by and told him how a white manager had

SUCCESS SECRETS OF BLACK EXECUTIVES

thrown a tantrum upon hearing that Smith was passed over. With the knowledge that he had an ally, Smith nurtured the relationship with the manager and eventually rose through the organization.

But the networking was just beginning for Coleman and Smith. As we mentioned, Silicon Graphics Inc. was one of the few American publicly-trade companies to have two blacks among its senior executives.

It is not coincidental that Marc Hanna, then a doctoral student in electrical engineering at Stanford University, was a member of the original group of eight that founded Silicon Graphics Inc. Hanna, winner of the Black Engineer of the Year award, created the "Geometry Engine" integrated circuit as part of his doctoral dissertation that made the 3-dimensional scientific workstation possible.

Hanna, like other founding members, still works at the company as vice president/chief scientist of the Entry Systems Division. The founders all stayed in the technical realm, including chairman James Clark, their faculty advisor, and hired experienced managers to run the company.

Hanna's input was critical in spotlighting black executives like Coleman and Smith, who probably would not have risen to similar positions in the much-larger Hewlett Packard.

Coleman, known as the "godfather" to some, helped recruit a large number of engineering, marketing and general management managers to Hewlett Packard, which had the most aggressive affirmative action effort in Silicon Valley, where they proved their mettle and moved into the start-up companies that flourished throughout Silicon Valley.

Coleman, Smith and others created links between Bay Area university programs, professional organizations, established companies and the venture capitalists that both fund and staff startups that moved African-American executives in Silicon Valley into positions unprecedented in American business.

It was an achievement that rebounded in their own favor when Silicon Graphics Inc. was created.

FROM THE EDITORS OF ASPIRE

The corporate environment is a cut-throat world particularly in the current economic marketplace.
One of the critical lessons of these pioneering African-American executive is the importance of establishing effective networks.
Smith got more proof when he decided to leave SGI.

"I want to make lots of money."

"Don't let anybody fool you about why they're an entrepreneur," says Howard Smith. "I'm in this because I want to make lots of money."
"I've done well in corporate life, but the real money is in your own company."
Smith was talking to a meeting of the Bay Area chapter of the National MBA association being held at Amdahl Corp.
"Twenty years ago Gene Amdahl had an office down the hall from mine at IBM," recalls to a shocked audience. "But he believed you could do something that everybody thought couldn't be done. He took on IBM and succeeded. Now all these buildings have his name on them."
Howard Smith has set out to make his name in workstation software.
Clarity Software, his one-year-old start-up raised $3 million in venture capital in 30 days, according to Smith.
"You know why?" he asks. "Because I convinced them that this was going to be the greatest company ever in software and that we're going to be a big company."
Smith has always believed in the power of networking.
However, even he was surprised by the response when he boldly launched a new software company in January 1990.
A host of industry veterans flocked to join Clarity Software Inc. and within one year they introduced their first product to rave reviews across the workstation market.
Clarity began 1991 in the position to achieve the same kind of market positioning as billion-dollar Microsoft has achieved in the

SUCCESS SECRETS OF BLACK EXECUTIVES

personal computer market.

Smith had become one of the highest ranking African-American executives in manufacturing as senior vice president-engineering for Silicon Graphics Inc. in Mountain View, California. However, he recognized a need for software solutions for the workstations SGI was building.

"I was very fortunate having been with a company that has been very successful for both me and the company," Smith notes. "But you get to the stage where you just want to test your own wings."

His marketplace is technical workstation users, whose terminals carry out such applications as computer-aided design or computer-aided manufacturing. However the power of these computers is of little use when they need to create a report on their work. Often they had to sit a personal computer next to the workstation for more general applications.

On Jan. 22, 1991, Clarity -- one year earlier, one man with an idea -- unveiled Rapport, one program that includes a document editor, spreadsheet, presentation graphics, advanced electronic mail and support for sound and facsimile.

The reviews were highly positive.

"Clarity Rapport will be an exciting product," says Ed McCracken, president of Silicon Graphics Inc. "This product supports customers' needs to present ideas visually in the 90s. Rapport's seamless incorporation of images and graphics reinforces our experience that visual processing conveys far more information than text alone."

"Rapport is a great example of how a developer can exploit the Sun environment to provide an innovative, easy-to-use productivity tool for everyday use," says Ed Zander, vice president of corporate marketing at Sun Microsystems. "It will be included in our CDware program which lets users try out and buy software from their office."

John Vigeland, an office automation specialist in New Jersey, says, "The graphical and multi-media promise of UNIX workstations has finally been fulfilled by an electronic messaging system, Clarity Rapport. UNIX workstation users can now share ideas in a compound document format, like their PC LAN brethren have been doing for years."

Even before product introduction, Clarity has entered strategic alliances with Sun, Digital Equipment, Hewlett Packard, Network Computing Devices, Silicon Graphics and SPARC International.

"We were the rage at Uniforum," beamed Smith following the product introduction during the leading trade show for UNIX applications and hardware.

The significance of that broad appeal requires some background on UNIX, an operating system developed by AT&T in the 1970s that has become an industry standard for multi-user workstations. However, practically every manufacturer has developed their own brand of UNIX. Over the past few years, rival coalition of manufacturers have banded together to create industry-wide standards.

Despite all the smoke and fire, no one had gotten past the operating system to design any software other than "vertical" programs designed for specific applications.

Into that void stepped Smith, at the same time, at the same time that workstation prices had dropped to be competitive with high-end personal computers.

Gwen Peterson, Clarity's vice president of marketing, says Rapport, "helps bring workstations into the computer mainstream. With hardware prices comparable to PC's and easy-to-use productivity applications now available, more user will choose UNIX workstations for the extra capabilities they offer. And with Rapport's ability to share fully-formatted compound documents with Macs and PC's, workstation users become full participants in corporate-wide mail networks."

In short, his product has the opportunity to be a fixture not only on engineering desktops but in a whole range of business computing environments.

The pacesetting role is not a new one to Smith. He was one of the early African-American engineers to work in Silicon Valley in the late 1960s. At that time, they could only live in east San Jose. "In fact, there was one apartment building on East Santa Clara Street where practically all the black engineers in the valley lived when they first moved out here," he recalls.

He has also reached out to network throughout Silicon Valley, developing an national reputation for his skill and integrity. Those relationships helped him raise sizable venture capital in Silicon Valley, which greatly aided his ability to go from idea stage to product launch in a year's time.

PCWorld magazine selected Smith as one of the top 20 computer industry executives in 1991, on a list with Microsoft's Bill Gates, Apple's John Sculley and Sun's Scott McNealy.

As a result, he's on the dinner circuit to break bread with those captains of industry, expanding his network and his horizons even further.

His success also brings a geometric increase in the opportunities available to other African-American executives. Chuck Robinson, a colleague from Hewlett Packard days, is vice president of engineering, and Jim Lawrence, a Silicon Graphics alumnus, is chief financial officer of Clarity, which will probably pass the $100 million mark within two years.

The history of Silicon Valley is filled with examples of early-stage African-American executives paving the way for others to follow.

Any executive of any race who tries to survive as an island by themselves is doomed to extinction.

Sisters Are Doing It

When the burdens of the job overwhelm Dottie Robinson, a product distribution coordinator at Hewlett Packard Co., she can pick up the phone and call Mary Sutton, a software manager at Lockheed Missiles and Space Co, or Fran Traylor, a marketing analyst with GTE.

All three belong to Women for Positive Communications, a networking group that began in 1974 among Lockheed employees and expanded to bring in members from other Silicon Valley companies.

FROM THE EDITORS OF ASPIRE

"The networking is the key for me," said Traylor. "The group allows me the opportunity to interact with other businesswomen."

WPC president Janice Parkinson says, "When we founded it at Lockheed, we felt there was a need for a support system." The group has also allowed the members to project themselves into the community. During its monthly dinner meetings, speakers such as Superior Court Judge LaDoris Cordell keep them abreast of current affairs. WPC also supports charities and provides scholarships.

Their group is not an isolated phenomenon. African-American employees at many of the Bay Area's major employees have banded together into networks, either formal or informal.

Charlie Harris, community programs manager at International Business Machines Corp. in San Jose, says, "We do keep in touch and as people move around, often someone will tell them, 'when you get to San Jose, get in touch with Charlie Harris and he'll let you know what's going on." However, there is not a formal organization. An ad hoc group has mounted a Martin Luther King Jr. Day lunch each year for the past five years.

In contrast, the Bay Area Black Employees at Xerox Corp. is part of a national network sanctioned by the highest levels of the company. Majuana Martin, an Oakland-based account executive heads the group. "Our organization covers San Francisco, Sacramento, Oakland and Santa Clara."

Despite corporate support, such groups can run into resistance, Martin noted. "Our CEO supports us and he's well aware of what we're doing, but we've had some whites complain about BABE. But when we have events, we had nothing to hide and everyone was invited."

Each Xerox region has a Black Caucus comprised of employee networks like BABE, and the national black employees group has a yearly convention.

An example of the entrenched ethnocentric resistance came from Intel Corp. president Andrew Grove, author of best-selling books on management and a weekly newspaper Q&A column on management. In 1987, he received a question from a white worker

Success Secrets of Black Executives

who complained about her black boss recruiting other black employees to join a black employee organization. When she complained to the boss' supervisor, the supervisors backed the boss' efforts. The questioner said her boss' activities were divisive.

Grove agreed with the questioner and opposed the black employee organization on the grounds of "workplace relevance." He urged the employee to quit if the supervisors did not take action against her boss.

When the editor of the San Jose Business Journal responded to Grove, charging that had Grove replaced "black organization" with United Way or engineering society, that his answer would be different, and that he would never encourage an employee to go around a white boss, Grove was unrepentant. They dueled over the issue in competing columns for six weeks, but Grove, a Hungarian immigrant who had found his American dream in Silicon Valley, never "got it."

Apple Computer Inc. workers formed the Apple Black Networking Association to help sensitize their company to its diverse workforce. Co-chairs are Denise Coley, Barron Cox and Paula McClain. Coley said the group has already helped bring about a new equal opportunity program and the hiring of an African-American vice president, Bernard Gifford, former dean of graduate education at the University of California, Berkeley.

ABNA helped sponsor receptions for both Gifford and Santiago Rodriquez, the new affirmative action officer. In addition to monthly meetings, members can keep track of each other through the company's electronic mail system which has an address for the association.

"Both within and outside the company, we want to make people aware there is a true diversity at Apple," says Coley. The group launched a tradition of a holiday Kwanza gathering and helped encourage participation on the Freedom Train for Martin Luther King Jr.'s birthday.

Also launched was B.E.S.T., the Black Employee Society for a Better Tomorrow at FMC Corp. in Santa Clara. Roy Davis, Don

FROM THE EDITORS OF ASPIRE

Williams and Charles Brown head that group which meets monthly. They've brought in representatives of similar networks from Pacific Bell and from the South Bay Urban Bankers Association.

"Because of different shifts and different buildings, we've got people who've been here 15 years and don't know each other," says Williams. "We just want to know who is who and who is where so we can keep each other aware of opportunities."

Internal advancement is a recurring theme among the different associations. Unlike area-wide professional groups, these company networks create lines of communication about new jobs, company benefits and events that can give their members an edge.

Martin says such groups can also help employees in trouble. "If a person is put on disciplinary action, they should have a place to go to find out how to solve that problem."

SUCCESS SECRETS OF BLACK EXECUTIVES

FROM THE EDITORS OF ASPIRE

VI
INTERNATIONAL EXPERIENCE

"Asians would rather deal with Black Americans than white Americans because whites usually won't take the time to understand their culture and their economy."

Will Bass, President, Ivory Integrated Technology
built first American factories to operate in the People's
Republic of China and the Soviet Union

Will Bass and Ivory Integrated Technology are ready for the world economy.

Fresh off setting up a computer assembly plant in Moscow, he just led a trade mission from the State of California to Zimbabwe and Nigeria comprised of 10 African-American companies in search of deals.

It was his second trip to African on behalf of California and Bass thinks the continent is ripe for doing business. "We're now working on a joint venture in Zimbabwe with Plessy," says Bass.

"Another entrepreneur from Sacramento is involved in building a massive housing development in Zimbabwe," he adds.

Bass has thought globally for more than 10 years while participating in a half billion dollars worth of joint ventures, strategic alliances and acquisitions.

His 5,000 square foot headquarters in Fremont is linked to his second office in Hong Kong. "We're opening a third office in Abajian, Ivory Coast before the year is out."

Bass also launched Eagle Chemical to distribute chemical products to industry. "It's growing pretty rapidly, and we're going to have to add space to accommodate it."

The Hong Kong office is positioned to handled deals in the People's Republic of China and the rest of the Pacific Rim. Bass has handled two joint manufacturing ventures from Fortune 500 firms in the PRC. Combined with his computer deal in the Soviet Union, Bass is well placed to take advantage of the opening economies of the communist world.

The technology entrepreneur moved into his own business after rising to be a vice president at Storage Technologies Inc. He was a specialist in marketing semiconductors and electronic components.

However, his portfolio has expanded through Ivory. The company has done ventures in agriculture, textiles, electronics and oil. Bass was even approached about handling imports of African art to the Bay Area.

Despite the far flung nature of his business, Bass still finds time for his community. A trustee of Oakland's progressive Allen Temple Baptist Church, Bass helped found 100 Black Men of the Bay Area. Its goal include promoting entrepreneurship, creating networks between businesspeople and encouraging scholarship among young African-Americans.

Opportunity in Japanese

Jamaican immigrant Leo M. Wilson cast his entrepreneural eye on the tremendous commercial real estate market in Silicon Valley, but wondered to find a source of capital for his commercial mortgage brokerage.

The answer came to him in Japanese.

"Most of the investment capital was coming from Japan, but none of the developers here spoke Japanese," recalled Wilson. "So I invested the time in learning Japanese."

As a result, Wilson arranged the largest commercial real estate transaction in th e history of Silicon Valley, a $10 0 million retail and apartment complex at the intersection of U.S. 101 and Lawrence Expressway built by Trammell Crow Partners, the biggest U.S. development firm.

"The Japanese needed someone who not only understood them, but could represent their interests," adds Wilson. Oddly, gaining entry to the top financial interests in Tokyo and Osaka while speaking a second language was easier than overcoming racism in the United States.

"Even though I had the capital to put deals together, early on, people wouldn't take me seriously. There's a skyscraper near San Francisco that had been on the market for years, when I called the owner and made an offer for $50 million. Then I showed up, and he was totally unprepared. He wanted to back out, but once I put the funds on the table, we did the deal."

Success Secrets of Black Executives

FROM THE EDITORS OF ASPIRE

VII
CREATIVITY

"Day after day, week after week, this message -- that black America is dysfunctional and unwhole -- gets transmitted across the American landscape. Sadly, as a result, America never learns the truth about what is a wonderful, vibrant, creative community of people."
Denver-based journalist Patricia Raybon in My Turn column
Newsweek, Oct. 2, 1989

Carol Williams of Carol H. Williams Advertising Agency ha s a wonderfully lucrative knack for focusing her clients' products in the best possible light. In 19 years, Williams flair and expertise in advertising has harvested massive profits for the manufacturers and organizations she promotes and a reputation as a superior advertising professional.

As the creator of the advertising campaign for Kentucky Fried Chicken's Finger Likin' Good" and Secret's "Strong Enough for a Man, But Made for a Woman," its crystal clear why Williams' brilliance as an advertising agency principal is revered.

Ironically, Williams really hadn't considered advertising as a permanent career even while employed at Leo Burnett Advertising, the Chicago-based agency noted for transforming a fledgling Minnesota canning company into Green Giant.

"I thoroughly loved writing and reading at the time, but I really hadn't considered advertising at all as a career," notes Williams who is finally working on her first novel.

Twenty years ago, Williams took a summer internship for Leo Burnett while a student at Northwestern University. There her talent for pithy, stylized copy. Fortunately, for Williams, Burnett and her clients such as KFC, Secret and Pillsbury, she was offered a permanent position.

SUCCESS SECRETS OF BLACK EXECUTIVES

After 11 years for Burnett, Williams decided to explore advertising West Coast style and accepted a position with Foote Cone and Belding in San Francisco.

Not long afterward, Williams formed Carol H. Williams Advertising Agency of Oakland, with a client roster including Lotus Development, Pacific Bell, the California Lottery, Gallo Salami, Clorox and Oakland International Airport.

The secret to her success has been to write advertising copy that gives the reader or viewer the sensations of the product. With the Pillsbury "Dough Boy", her campaign conveys the joy of a child enjoying the home-cooked baked products.

The KFC "Finger Lickin' Good" ads almost make one smack their lips and pick their teeth as the taste of the chicken is triggered.

The Secret campaign addresses the female concern that deodorants geared to their market were not strong enough.

In most of her creative endeavors, being an African-American woman has brought new perspectives that traditional agency professionals might not consider. Her success is all the more notable because the advertising industry has one of the worst employment records for minorities of all major industries, with fewer than two percent minority employees, according to industry bible Advertising Age.

Williams has done television, print, billboards and direct mail marketing. "Since we specialized in all forms of marketing in every aspect of media for their product or organization," she notes. "Basically, we provide strategic advertising with a creative edge."

Her focus is on general market accounts, geared to the general public. Some are target market accounts, however some companies are worried about the controversy of having special promotions for specific audiences.

"Target marketing is becoming a big issue because white companies are beginning to look seriously at the liability of target marketing. Not only are consumers hurt but black ad agencies lose as well."

For the moment, however, with accounts established in

technology, household products, transportation and food industries, Williams ' next goal is securing a major auto account.

But, she has not lost track of her ambition. She's adamant about finishing her first novel, which she hints, may bear a resemblance to her experiences within the advertising industry.

Success Secrets of Black Executives

FROM THE EDITORS OF ASPIRE

VIII
RISK TAKING

"A lot of that (an obsession with security among black workers) had to do with an assessment of opportunities. There was a feeling that you only got one or two chances. Now that you got this far, let's not mess it up. If you took a risk, sometimes there's the feeling that you couldn't overcome that."

Joe Avery, Vice President-Operations
Adept Technologies Inc.

Vivian Cole was not one to let opportunity knock twice.

As an employee of Technology Development Corp. in 1984, she was offered a chance to acquire its contract to provide technical support to a National Aeronautics and Space Administration facility in the San Joaquin Valley.

It was the beginning of Fremont-based Synernet, which now provides a variety of technology services to government and industry.

In addition to that original contract, which involves operating a test facility for Vertical Takeoff and Landing Aircraft, Synernet also has contracts with the U.S. Air Force to build a life cycle cost data base for avionics systems.

Synernet's 30 employees work in four locations, Fremont, Mountain View, San Joaquin and Arizona.

Jacob Adams, Synernet executive vice president, said the firm is seeking more diversity in its customer base due to the declining federal budget. "Often, when times get tight, big contractors will bring in-house functions they had contracted out. For small business, it's a matter of maintaining what you have."

It's a time when contracts awarded under the Small Business Administration's Section 8(a) program can be invaluable. The SBA encourages federal agencies to find contracts which are restricted for award to small, disadvantaged businesses. In that way, smaller companies get the opportunity to build experience without the advantage that larger, better-capitalized companies have in normal bidding.

However, the requirements to participate are strenuous. Detailed applications list the company's financial status, organization, business plan, resumes of key staff and operating manuals. Then, companies are graduated out of the program after a certain time in 8(a) or after reaching a certain size.

"Nothing is given to you," says Adams. "You have to go the program and sell them that the job can be done better by a small business and get them to set it aside."

Synernet is also looking at acquisitions and at technology transfer from area universities. "The State of California has a new program to encourage more technology transfer from our universities to small business," adds Adams. "I get the sense that there is a lot of valuable research that goes unused by the commercial sector."

Forging into those new directions is risky, but Synernet has learned to manage risk. It has also learned that building a business can not occur without taking risks.

FROM THE EDITORS OF ASPIRE

IX
TIME MANAGEMENT

"No one controls your time. It's just a matter of determining your habits of time management.
                                    Management consultant Pat Johnson

A busy schedule does not have to be an uncontrolled schedule, according to management consultant Rick Griggs. He says people who discover how much time they waste can then use that time to work more productively, support their social concerns and enjoy life more.

"Most of us need work in time management in both our work and our personal life," says Griggs. "The classic time wasters are the telephone, failure to set priorities, crises and interruptions."

Pat Johnson, a productivity specialist, targets the "Three P's: Procrastination, Patterns and Parasites" as enemies of those seeking to control their schedules. "People fall into a time trap and feel that some external force is controlling your time."

Griggs agrees that people often spend too much time talking either in meetings, or on the phone. "The more you can settle an issue in one conversation, the better off you'll be. Playing telephone tag is a big time waster." For meetings, he gives clients a list of 13 suggestions to make meetings more effective.

"I was in a meeting with a large multi-million dollar organization that was paying three consultants and ten of its staff to attend a meeting that had no agenda, started late and the key people existed several times ," recalls Griggs.   "I wound up spending an hour on the phone each with two people who should have gotten the information at the meeting."

Johnson observes that otherwise-punctual professionals often think it's alright to show up late when they're among acquaintances.

Success Secrets of Black Executives

"I often have to say when I'm announcing a meeting that we're not starting on CP (colored people's) time. We have an atmosphere that it's okay. But the same people know they'd better not be late for church because that standard has been reinforced. One of the things we can do is to borrow from organizations like the Lions Club, that has fines and other kinds of sanctions to enforce promptness."

Procrastination is one of the primary topics Johnson discusses in her workshops. "The first thing is to admit it," she says. "There's a lot of denial that goes on with procrastination. It's like alcoholism and AA." By a self-evaluation procedure, she helps participants to diagnose their own patterns of procrastination. "It is like a disease, and I present it that way."

California Superior Court Judge LaDoris Hazzard Cordell of Palo Alto rarely has the luxury of procrastination as she balances her family, career and community interests. "The first thing for me is to be as organized as I can be on the home front," says the former Stanford law professor. "If things get crazy on the home front, it tends to carry over into everything else.

"There is a routine established that gives us structure. Six nights per week, we know what dinner is going to be, so we don't have to waste a half-hour worrying about it. It really helps when you're a single parent." Cordell also saves time by setting the table for breakfast each night before turning in.

Always close at hand is a large calendar that Cordell uses for her speaking engagements, meetings , caseload and activities for her children. It helps her set some priorities for her activities.

Setting a fee for her speaking engagements helped control that phase. "However, I do at least one free speaking engagement each month for some cause that's important to me." Cordell has also limited her board involvement to those agencies she finds critical, such as child abuse, the Urban League and the United Way.

Despite the elaborate planning, the time crunch often comes with personal time. "There are some times I just desperately want time to myself," says Cordell, a skilled tennis player and an accomplished singer and pianist.

Griggs says many professionals neglect the need for quality personal growth time. "It boils down to a problem of balance between the personal life and professional career. The professional career gets most of the time and many times we forget the good skills we use in our career in planning our personal life."

For instance, telephone management techniques can also work with personal calls. "You should initiate telephone calls when you're prepared and don't be afraid to make a list of things you want to discuss and there's nothing wrong with taking notes. By calling more often, you can keep the calls shorter."

Griggs also stresses separation between career and personal life. "I run my own business, but I make it a point not to work at home. When we know we can work extended hours, we use that as a copout for not being very effective during the work day."

The consultant cited music as one way to make the transition from work to home. "Sometimes, it's an intermediate stop like a bar, or you can make your last phone call of the day from the office a personal one," he suggests. "The ideal way is a nice jog, walk or bike ride."

Cordell says the 20-minute drive from office to home is a chance to make a transition from judge to mother. She'd love to jog when she comes home, "but when the kids haven't seen you all day long, it's hard for them to understand you turning around and heading out the door." Her daily exercise tends to be in the early morning.

Griggs also suggests that not only parents and spouses, but also singles in relationships should leverage their professional and leisure time. "As often as you can, bring your significant other into professional things like open houses and networking meetings. They may be bored, but at least they get a chance to see you in another light.

"In your health and fitness activities, select the types of things you can do with another person," he concludes.

Success Secrets of Black Executives

From The Editors of ASPIRE

X
Targeting a Niche

"Every job I had was breaking new ground and I never worked for one boss too long. Every time I got to the point that I learned all I could, another opportunity came along."

Kenneth A. Coleman, senior vice president, Silicon Graphics Inc.

For a man moving as fast as N. John Douglas, transportation analogies are effective ways to express ideas. So his conversation is sprinkled with talk of trains and planes.

However, his role model is the submarine.

"While you're underwater, you don't let the enemy know what you're doing," he says. "Then when things are going really great, you can come up for air and ride the waves. When they're really bad, you just go back underwater and fire torpedos."

Douglas, who became only the second black television station owners in the nation when he put Channel 48 on the air in San Jose, dropped below the surface when he sold the station to the Telemundo chain of Hispanic-formatted stations. It was a successful end to Douglas' gamble with television narrowcasting.

He used a format of business news to turn the UHF channel into a profitable venture in a market with 12 broadcast television stations.

"It was sad to let it go," says Douglas, "like giving up one's first child for marriage."

However, Douglas promised last year to stay in broadcasting, his fourth career. Douglas first came to the Bay Area as a scientist for Lockheed in the early 1960s.

Then he shifted to become a securities analyst, before joining Castle and Cooke as a strategic planner. While looking at acquisition opportunities for the company, he became convinced of

Success Secrets of Black Executives

the profitability of broadcasting and launched Channel 48.

It was not a straight line success. There were times when Douglas struggled to meet payrolls. His biggest crisis came on a day when one of the two Klystron tubes, the heart of the television station's transmission system, blew. The tubes cost $50,000 apiece. The next day, the other tube blew. Somehow, the station was able to return to the air.

Douglas began looking for the next trend in broadcasting. "It's like hitting a moving train. The communications industry is not a static industry. What train do I really want to catch? How long do I want to be on this train?

"So you spend some time looking at train schedules and find out how I can get a ticket," he continues. "Now the best train is one with a good cash flow. Last October (the stock market crash in 1987) scared a lot of people."

He looked at other television stations with the $17 million he sold Channel 48 for, but decided they faced too much competition form cable television. That left the forgotten medium, AM radio. "It's been going through a long rebuilding process, like Union Station," he notes. "But we can buy stations at a very low price, because people are not bidding up the price of stations.".

So, he has cast his fortunes with the old standby. Within two years, he built a chain that covers the entire state of California. The goal is simple -- to reach the limit of 12 AM and 12 FM stations under the umbrella of Douglas Broadcasting.

Douglas' financial savvy is evident in his programming choices. Most African-American owners of radio stations program their format for their own community, reflecting their social goals to add diversity to the market place and their familiarity with the audience.

However, programming a station is expensive requiring staff, recordings, studios, etc. Douglas has managed to increase diversity in broadcasting without building in excessive overhead.

Rather than providing his own announcers and programs financed buy advertising, he sells blocks of time to producers who can then program it as they see fit.

From The Editors of ASPIRE

For instance, his San Francisco station now provides Mandarin Chinese programming and his Los Angeles station has blocks of African-American gospel and Korean programs. His Sacramento station is the flagship for a network of motivational speakers. It plays tapes at the expense of the motivators.
It's so simple, it's diabolical.
Douglas' train has left the station.

"You Buy It Because You Have To"
When a Soviet submarine sank following failure of an electrical component, Roy Clay saw an immediate example of the value of his hi-pot testers.
"If they had tested their components with our equipment, it would not have gone under," notes Clay.
His company, Rod-L Electronics in Menlo Park, makes the only dielectric withstand equipment certified for Underwriters Laboratories testing.
"You buy it because you have to," he adds. That goes for any electrical equipment operated on 120- or 220-volt AC lines from computers to hair dryers. "Our big markets are office equipment, data processing, medical equipment and test and measurement manufacturers."
His customer list includes a big chunk of the Fortune 500 and U.S. government agencies such as NASA and the Departments of Defense and Energy. "Every product produced by AT&T, IBM, Hewlett Packard, Digital, Compaq and Apple, to name a few, is tested by a Rod-L tester on line. There's not a computer manufacturer we don't sell to."
The product line includes insulation resistance testers, ground continuity testers and dielectric withstand. Their use is to send electric overloads through equipment to determine if each individual product can withstand surges without electric surges, which can cause fires. To receive the Underwriters Laboratories certification, a requirement by most insurers for home or industrial equipment, such tests must be performed.
Clay got into the market because testing giant Hewlett-Packard,

where Clay headed the research that created its first computer systems in the 1960s, decided that the hi-pot testing market wouldn't grow quickly enough.

Hewlett-Packard decided to buy them from Clay rather than make them itself.

From that start, Rod-L expanded to each the remainder of the electronics industry.

Clay has coupled his business success with a strong civic responsibility. He was the only African-American city councilman in the history of Palo Alto and is still quite active in city and Democratic politics. He is a board member of the Community Development Institute of East Palo Alto, a force behind the city's incorporation and growth. When the Olympic Club of San Francisco opened its doors to African-American members, Clay was one of the first invited to join.

More quietly, Clay spends a lot of time in contact with African-American college students, particularly in science and business fields, helping them set career goals.

His own three sons are a source of pride. All work for Rod-L. Two are electrical engineers and one is a business student. "It's an opportunity for them to see all aspects of the business and I know they're committed."

FROM THE EDITORS OF ASPIRE

XI
KEEPING OPTIONS OPEN

"Once the company gets into play, the company is no longer in control. It becomes a bidding war."
Maurice Barron, retired vice president-finance and taxation
Safeway Inc.

During an open roundtable discussion on "surviving mergers and acquisitions," host Virginia Walker pointed out "The choices of corporate management (for mergers and acquisitions) may not coincide with your personal career options."

Almost everyone in the room had some personal experience with at least one side of a merger/acquisition.

Wendell Jones, vice president/chief financial officer of Infergene Inc. in Benecia, had just participated in the sale of the firm, where he was a founder, to a Swedish biomedical company. "We've already lost several members of our marketing staff who decided to leave."

Jones' assessment was that his job would probably be redundant after the deal was completed. However, Jones pointed out that the founders had planned to sell the company from the very beginning. His approach is to position himself to take advantage of other opportunities including his own company.

"Being realistic is really important," says Jones. "You have to have a plan A and a plan B and not feel so entrenched that you think you can't be replaced."

Walker suggested, "You have to assess the person at the comparable position to see where you and they stack up."

Glenn Toney, vice president-human resources of Applied Materials Inc. says, "If you can be realistic about yourself, you're starting at a very good point."

SUCCESS SECRETS OF BLACK EXECUTIVES

Russell Curtis, president of the Woodside Summit Group in Redwood City, says, "Either you have the skills or you don't. We have to have to compete at a very high level to get to this point."

Caretha Coleman, vice president/human resources of Software Publishing Corp., which ha s acquired several companies, says the corporate culture is another important consideration.

"You have to look at the type of organization you're merging with," she concludes.

FROM THE EDITORS OF ASPIRE

XII
INNOVATIVE SALES

"What they do is very easy to measure. They either sell or they don't."
                    Maurice Barron, retired vice president- finance and taxation, Safeway Inc.

It makes a difference that Tom Goss understands ethnic tastes. Within two years, he crafted a marketing strategy that appeals to "diverse tastes" while carving a solid niche against the marketing onslaught of cola giants Coca-Cola and PepsiCo.

"Everyone remembers how much we enjoyed sweet fruity drinks as youngsters," says Goss, executive vice president and general manager of ShasCo Corp. in Hayward.

"Well, ShasCo still makes those beverages and we also provide flavors that are not as sweet as our regular flavors."

Shasta's roots are in diet drinks. "We focus on one segment of our customers who prefer our diet drinks, mineral waters and citrus-based drinks," he points out. "And we have our regular line of 38 flavors to appeal to ethnic tastes."

For owner National Beverage Co. of Fort Lauderdale, Fla., ShasCo generated more than $70 million from 20 million cases of soft drinks, an increase of 20 percent during Goss' first two years at the helm.

His strategy is rooted in lessons learned at the age of 12. "It's not the business of beverages that I longed for, it's the business of sales and marketing. I started as a kid at 12 shining shoes. I had three others working for me then. I had to satisfy consumers then and have to satisfy them now."

After starring as a defensive end for the University of Michigan, where he received a degree in communications, Goss held sales

Success Secrets of Black Executives

management jobs for Proctor and Gamble. He then joined RJR Foods in Winston-Salem, N.C. and played a major role in R.J. Reynolds' merger with Del Monte.

Goss arrived in the Bay Area as Del Monte's vice president of sales for the western U.S. Next, Goss joined Faygo Corp. and found himself on the other side of an acquisition. However, the acquirer, National Beverage, launched a decentralization plan and placed Goss atop their ShasCo subsidiary in Hayward.

The executive has not stood pat. In addition to increasing production and flavors, he recently spearheaded the acquisition of A'Sante, a mineral water with juice added, from Anheuser Busch. The beverage is a direct competitor of Calistoga and other mineral water brands.

Niche marketing has been crucial to ShasCo's survival as a beverage company. Goss capitalized on the "cola war" to highlight Shasta's flavored drinks while downplaying its cola.

"Coke and Pepsi has just about driven everyone else out of the market. If you try to compete with them head on, you're asking for trouble," says Goss. "You have to remember their ability to pay for advertising and marketing. They have millions to spend."

Compared to the big players, ShasCo can only reach 50 percent of the beverage consuming market because of a different distribution pattern. However, that difference creates a marketing and price advantage.

"We're often asked, 'How can you price your beverages so low?'" says Goss. "We can because Shasta is the only warehouse brand. Our product is picked up from our warehouse by Lucky's, taken to their warehouse and distributed to their store in their trucks. Coke and Pepsi have their products delivered direct to stores by trucks owned to them. The difference in cost is clear."

The average Shasta six-pack costs $1.79 compared to $2.09 for the cola brands, according to industry sources.

The price advantage allows Shasta to focus on two distinct markets. "With our diet flavors, we target the more upscale consumer," says Goss.

"Our regular flavors are geared to our blue collar and ethnic tastes. Ethnic tastes tend to be sweeter," he adds. "Blacks, Asians and Hispanics tend to be younger. And when you were younger, you liked things more flavorful and fruity. We make 38 different flavors, but all are not available in the same market because flavors tend to be regional. And flavors appeal to different ethnicities. If you have a large black population, it will tend to prefer root beer, orange and grape."

Football helped teach Goss how to compete and he's found that it still creates good business instincts. He's "quite proud" of San Francisco 49er Keena Turner's role with ShasCo in advertising and marketing.

The company has on average 120 employees, a number that grows during the summer. "In the winter, we might have six people on the line, but 20 people in the summer, particularly in Northern California. The weather is more heavily skewed than in Southern California."

Goss has played tennis every week for the past 16 years and is a B level player. He has also taken up golf.

Yet, when most businesses are winding down for vacations, his business gets much hotter.

That's because he's selling the tastes of summer.

Goss' success is an indication of how sales and marketing can lead into the top executive posts. As Safeway's Maurice Barron projects, marketing executives have the best path to reach the chief executive's spot.

It worked for Lalita Tademy, president of Alps Electric U.S.A. in San Jose. She joined the computer printer manufacturer as vice president of marketing. She decided to develop a new market segment in an area her supervisors were not interested in. Working on her own time, she landed "a major piece of business" that has resulted in excess of $50 million in new sales.

Tony Merritt is another sales pacesetter. He was the first African-American to head a sales region for Toyota Motor Sales Co. as northern California district manager. He responded by leading his 55

SUCCESS SECRETS OF BLACK EXECUTIVES

dealers to new sales records during years when car sales declined nationwide. The market share in Merritt's region is 50 percent higher than Toyota sales nationally and 60 percent higher for small trucks.

"We've got the jump on the competition," he quips, repeating an advertising slogan. The ability to increase market share was critical because of the declining auto market. "With the products Toyota has, our dealers can make gains in profitability and penetration."

Merritt had been national merchandising manager of Toyota Motor Distributors. He had served as assistant manager of the Denver region after a decade working for Ford Motor Co.

The differences between the American and Japanese automakers are apparent to Merritt. "The management style is different," he notes. "Here(at Toyota), things flow from the bottom up. There, things flow from the top down. Here, things get reviewed through the lower levels of management so that when they get to the top, they've been well thought out. With the domestics, it starts at the top and you get involved after the fact."

FROM THE EDITORS OF ASPIRE

XIII
Enjoyment

The four-question test for accepting a job:
- *Will I grow and learn?*
- *Is it visible?*
- *Is it important to the company?*
- *And will I enjoy it?*

If these are true, then it's a good thing for you to take.

Kenneth A. Coleman, senior vice president, Silicon Graphics Inc.

Hit, hit, hit, hit...
The hit records keep rolling off the assembly line of Narada Michael Walden's music factory in San Rafael.
Will it ever stop?
Check out the hook...
"I never wanted to be typecast," says Marin County's most famous Grammy-winning producer. "I have produced a lot of female singers, but that's because they're cute. I love beautiful women," he chuckles with a light rolling laughter like the waves coming in from the coast.
As that wave washes back out, Walden tells how seriously he listens to the competition. "I'm like a football coach. If George Seifert(San Francisco 49ers head coach) has not done his homework, then there's no way they're ready for the (next team). I'm always listening to what radio is playing. These kids are throwin' these days."
Walden, whose musical roots go back to the Woodstock generation and the Mahavishnu Orchestra, is throwin' a record a week from Perfection Light Productions, which in ten years has become one of

Success Secrets of Black Executives

the Bay Area's African-American owned businesses.

Just in recent weeks, his visitors have included Whitney Houston and the O'Jays. For Houston, he produced her new album.

"They come to me to make hits. I give them hits."

Like Mahavishnu in the 1960s, Walden believes in maintaining the cutting edge on the musical scene. "You've got to figure it takes three to four months to hit the street after you leave the studio, so you have to be out ahead of what's happening now." That's the approach for his dance tracks.

"Now for ballads, there's always a special feeling for something soulful and heart-stirring just as long as its passionate enough. It's got to be something that the people in the car will be moved by."

From Aretha to Pia Zadora, Narada has been the preferred producer over the past 10 years. However, it all started because he couldn't fit into Quincy Jones' schedule to get his own album produced.

Washington, D.C. teenager Stacy Lattisaw became his first client. "I knew Herb Allen with Cotillion (Records) was looking for a producer and I offered to do four sides and if they liked it, then the whole album. The result was "Let Me Be Your Angel."

After the hit, the phone never stopped ringing. Before long, his career as a musician had faded into the background. "Now, I've got to produce to pay the bills. I've got this big studio and all."

Depending on the project, Walden's staff ranges from "the A Team of about 20 people, the B Team of about 40 people and then there's the C Team of another 60 that come in and have pizza and hang out."

It's his joking way of relating to being a big business. On the serious tip, Walden jealously guards his independence. "I can't predict where the next hit is coming from. I have to be free to do what I like."

He regrets not taking on Jasmine Guy's debut album. "If she asks me again, I will work with her. I'd set it up so she'd just have to step in...like premeditated murder, you know...ha..ha..ha..ha. A producer can make a person like Jasmine sound fabulous. Does anyone talk about Paula Abdul being a good singer. No, but they put it together

FROM THE EDITORS OF ASPIRE

and it sounds good."

But, whatever the decision, it's Walden's choice along with brother Kevin and manager Clarence Avant in Los Angeles. "If you work with one company, then they take advantage of you."

Avant handles the Hollywood scene for Walden. "I only go down when I have to."

He's at home on the Marin coast. "I start every day with a five-mile run. Then I go play some tennis. By the time I hit the studio, I'm pumpin.'"

He shol' is.

XIV
SELF-EVALUATION

"I know people don't want to hear it, but my advice is to be patient. It doesn't always happen as fast as you want it to."
Lalita Tademy, President, Alps Electric U.S.A.

As mentioned, African-American executives have a problem getting reliable feedback about their performance. Their fish bowl environment can magnify both successes and failures. That's why honest self-evaluation and close support from mentors is critical.

"There are always preconceived ideas about you," says Bob Sanders, president of AlphaNumeric executive search firm, "and you don't want to give anyone the opportunity to use them against you. Evaluate the situation you're in and determine what moves you have to make."

"You've got to learn how to read people," says Sanders. "If the boss likes to fish, then you need to go fishing. People tend to promote people they like."

Part of the self-assessment is an evaluation of one's growth strategy. "My achievement has been a combination of my own performance and having the opportunity to have that performance viewed by people in a decision-making position," notes Glenn Toney, vice president-human resources at Applied Materials.

"The real preparation was going outside the scope of the jobs I had," recalls Joe Avery, vice president-operations of Adept Technologies. "I spent a lot of time operating well outside the sphere."

"The goals I set personally were short term," adds Avery. "When I first went to Hewlett-Packard, my biggest goal was to make $1,000 a month. Maybe a shift supervisor. Then I had a mentor--Matt Schmutz--saying I should reach for a higher goal. That counseling really helped."

FROM THE EDITORS OF ASPIRE

"There are probably a lot more blacks in the valley who are capable of filling top management posts than have the capability to do so," says Tim Harris, vice president-human resources of Novell Inc. "Often they have not had the opportunity at lower levels of management to have some of those experiences. Those experiences definitely take away a lot of the roadblocks."

SUCCESS SECRETS OF BLACK EXECUTIVES

FROM THE EDITORS OF ASPIRE

VX
MEASURABILITY

"I'm skeptical of jobs in which you can't figure out the responsibility from the title."

Jim Williams, chief financial officer, Tegal Corp.
Chairman, National Association of Corporate Treasurers

When IBM's Joe Gordon made the first measurement of the atomic structure of a metal surface underwater after midnight in a n upstate New York lab, he was too exhausted to celebrate.

There was still lots of data collection to do for Gordon and his research team from IBM's Almaden Research Center in San Jose.

The six-member team and a physicist from the University of Puerto Rico had devoted six years to using one of the world's most powerful X-rays to discover the pattern that one-molecule thick copper makes when deposited on a layer of silver.

As a result of that discovery, Gordon and partner Owen Melroy won an 1988 IBM Outstanding Technical Achievement Award. On Feb. 22, Gordon received the Engineer of the Year award from the Conference of Deans of Historically Black Colleges and Universities.

"Prior to this, there were no real methods for finding out what's on the surface and where it actually lay," says Gordon, manager of interfacial chemistry and structure at Almaden. "Now, it's largely guesswork."

One of the key manufacturing processes from IBM and other semiconductor makers is deposition of metals on surfaces to create integrated circuits and printed circuit boards. If it sounds simple, keep in mind that this is all happening at the submicron (one millionth of a meter) level.

It is the latest building block in a foundation that Gordon has built over the last 15 years at Almaden. "First, we came up with techniques for weighing materials, then the interfacial spectrum of what species are on the surface, and now how it's arranged."

Conducting tests *in situ*, or under water, is important because electroplating takes place in a solution.

Gordon's group spent many long nights at the Stanford Linear Accelerator Center in Menlo Park and at the Cornell High Energy Synchotron Source in New York, firing an X-ray one million times more powerful than the standard 18-volt laboratory X-ray at copper and lead deposited on silver.

Their experiment used two processes: X-ray absorption and X-ray diffraction.

Under the absorption technique, the researchers determined position of atoms by monitoring the absorption pattern for the X-ray. "It gets absorbed by the first atom," says Gordon.

Through diffraction, the researchers measured the angle at which the rays bounced off the surface to determine the distance between different atoms.

The discovery generated new demands for articles in technical books such as the Journal of the American Chemical Society and Surface Science, along with lectures around the world. "This is quite exciting for electrochemists," concludes Gordon.

FROM THE EDITORS OF ASPIRE

XVI
MENTORING

We caught Dr. Walter Massey on a Monday morning following his return from Camp David.

"It was our introductory meeting for the President's Council of Science Advisors," he recalled. "There were three topics that the President was particularly interested in: science education, global warming and science and economic development."

That kind of meeting has become commonplace for the Hattiesburg, Miss. native who got his start from a chance decision to help his mother drive some other students to take a scholarship qualifying test. While he was there, he took the test also.

Once he won the Ford Foundation award, Massey whizzed into Morehouse College as a high school junior and hasn't looked back since.

The nuclear physician thinks his own introduction to the sciences makes a point about how many other young African-American can make it in technology.

"There are 300 black Ph.d in physics, which is a growing number, but certainly not enough," said Massey. "What it means is that when the right circumstances exist, we can make it. So we have to work on creating the right circumstances."

Massey is in position to help that occur on several levels. As a powerful role model, he has become chair of the American Association for the Advancement of Science (AAAS), the nation's largest scientific organization.

SUCCESS SECRETS OF BLACK EXECUTIVES

He also sits atop one of the nation's research powerhouses as professor of physics and vice president for research and Argonne National Laboratories of the University of Chicago.

However, he is at heart a physicist, probing into many body theories of quantum liquids and solids.

Two professors guided him into that esoteric field of endeavor. "I had two mentors, both white, which means that you don't have to be a minority to mentor one. The first was Dr. S.H. Christensen, my professor at Morehouse College who really made me interested in physics. The second was my Ph.d advisor Dr. Eugene Feinberg at Washington University in St. Louis. I had tried several other advisors and hadn't had much success with finding a research topic. He suggested this line of research."

The result was Massey's rise to head the Argonne National Laboratories, home of some of the world's most advanced nuclear research. He joined the labs in 1966 as a postdoctoral fellow and became a staff physicist in 1968. After a stint at Brown University as Professor of Physics and Dean of the College, Massey returned to Argonne as director in 1979.

In 1982, he was named vice president for research of the University of Chicago in addition. In 1984, he gave up the lab director's post to concentrate on his university duties.

His new appointment as a presidential science advisor is the latest of a number of boards he serves on, including Amoco Corp., First National Bank of Chicago, Motorola Inc., Continental Materials Corp., the Tribune Co., Brown University, the Rand Corp. and the founding chair of the Chicago High Tech Association.

However, he is quick to point out that there are lots of Walter Masseys out there waiting to be discovered, not only in the United States.

Massey praised a number of programs that expose minority youth at an early age to science.

"Without singling out any one program, anything that lets our young people know early the importance of mathematics and science is good because those are the prerequisites for engineering careers."

FROM THE EDITORS OF ASPIRE

However, his desire to find new sources of engineers extend across the Atlantic. He heads the AAAS' Sub-Saharan Scientific Initiative, which has forged bonds between African and American scientists.

"One of the problems has been access to Western scientific journals, because those countries have limited hard foreign currency, so we've made it possible for their scientists to buy those journals in their currency at a discount," he said.

"We've also helped in the formation of several scientific societies, mostly multi-disciplinary," Massey added. "The two most important are the African Academy of Sciences and the Pan African Association of Science and Technology."

To foster more personal links, a yearly meeting between African and American scientists is being planned. "The next one will probably be in Zimbabwe," he adds.

So Massey, who owes his career to the influence of mentors, is a living representation of how to extend the highest levels of technology and scientific policy to African-Americans.

Success Secrets of Black Executives

FROM THE EDITORS OF ASPIRE

XVII
THE CORPORATE ENVIRONMENT

"The civil rights movement back in the 1960s and 1970s was an impetus in getting people in. However, the corporate atmosphere didn't change much. I don't see enough people coming in behind us."
                Maurice Barron, retired vice president-finance & taxation, Safeway Inc.

A color-blind society could be the worst scenario for fully integrating minority group members into the mainstream of American life.

Experts who forecast the America of tomorrow point out that our society will become increasingly diverse in its mix of cultures, but the trend of the last dozen years of conservative administrations and a conservative Supreme Court has been to treat everyone alike.

A San Francisco personnel management expert has gained fame for insisting that the color-blind approach will not integrate mostly lily-white power centers.

"I firmly believe the reason the "glass ceiling" exists is that none of us is comfortable talking about actual cultural differences that exist," says Lewis Griggs, president of Copeland Griggs Productions. "If that isn't discussed, there's no breaking the ice."

The "glass ceiling" describes the invisible barriers preventing minority group and women employees from rising beyond entry-level or low-level management positions once they break into the workforce.

Griggs, quick to note that he is a "Midwestern-born white male Stanford University M.B.A.," has produced a film series "Valuing Diversity" with the help of 30 major corporations. The newest films are "Supervising Differences, Champions of Diversity and Profiles in Change."

SUCCESS SECRETS OF BLACK EXECUTIVES

The series began with films on "Managing Differences, Diversity at Work, and Communicating Across Cultures." A fourth film shows entry-level employees how to get along with people who are different from themselves. It is called "You Make the Difference."

"The discovery of my own ethnocentrism led me into the field," says Griggs. "It meant I was ineffective outside my own culture. Statistically, the largest number of people in management positions are white males. The average white male doesn't even know there are differences. He has not had more than three times in his whole life occasions where he noticed that he was out of place; that his lifestyle was different and that he had to change it in order to be tolerated."

The result is often rejection based on the notion of "fit", said George Whaley, management professor in the School of Business at San Jose State University. "The buzz word in the valley in the 1980s was that you don't 'fit.' Once has to challenge a manager to measure 'fit.' More often than not, it's a sophisticated way to avoid measurement."

"California will be a mostly minority state by the year 2000," adds Whaley. "But it still means to most CEOs (chief executive officers) that the bottom of their corporation will change and not the top."

John Hill, equal opportunity officer for Rolm Systems, a unit of Siemens Corp. in Santa Clara, and chairman of the Santa Clara Valley Urban League, says the excuse for not hiring or promoting African-Americans used to be that we weren't educated; then they said we weren't trained; now they say we don't 'fit' no matter what the qualifications."

A 1989 survey by Impact Resources Inc. commissioned by Electron Access Inc. bears out Hill's points. Approximately 56 percent of the African-Americans in the Bay Area over 14 years of age have attended college, about the same percentage as the general population (see chart).

More than a fourth, 27.4 percent, hold managerial and professional jobs, twice the percentage that hold clerical or factory jobs.

Whaley developed the first course in affirmative action at San Jose

FROM THE EDITORS OF ASPIRE

State University more than a decade ago and has trained many of the human resources personnel now making decisions at Silicon Valley companies. He has also served as consultant to major corporations in the Bay Area.

Despite a backlash toward affirmative action in the media and in the courts, Whaley still firmly believes, "Discrimination is the problem, not affirmative action."

Griggs says most managers need to learn how to filter out institutional bias in their organizations. "The company should decide that there are certain things that are required to work here and get rid of the things that you think are not part of the 'fit' but part of the cultural style. As long as the achievement is there, all those things should be totally unimportant. A wise company would not only tolerate non-fitting styles but value different styles."

Bob Stenhouse, human resources manager for the California Teachers Association, says, "To really be effective, you have to change the social fabric of the company to eliminate racism and make management accountable for upholding the new value system.

"Affirmative action has worked, to the extent of our gaining access to jobs, but we're now talking about how to gain access to higher levels," adds Stenhouse. "Affirmative action is now taking on another meaning -- of full integration within the corporate structure.

Stenhouse mentioned an African-American lawyer in line for the job of CTA chief counsel several years ago. The lawyer was ruled out for the job, not over expertise, but over a fear that he would not be accepted in the social circles the job would take him into.

Now, after sensitivity training for the chief executive officer, African-Americans hold both the chief counsel and the governmental affairs slots, both requiring extensive public contact.

But for every chief executive with a new orientation, there are thousands clinging to notions such as "they don't fit."

Hill says, "That's why a lot of African-American people in corporations have stress and attendance problems. They're coming into my office ready to tear the walls down. When black males come into my office and start to cry, you know things are bad."

SUCCESS SECRETS OF BLACK EXECUTIVES

Griggs agrees that institutions must change as their workforce changes. "Affirmative action must continue, but affirmative action is not enough. To act affirmatively and then to leave them, means they will fail; they will fall away; and they will be perceived as having failed because of incompetence. They are feeling the effects of the glass ceiling and it's getting pretty heavy these days."

"Valuing Diversity" found the most acceptance from area technology firms. San Francisco's financial district has resisted the concept the most.

"The only way the financial district has any sense of it (diversity) is the foreign aspect because they deal with international transactions; they think money is the common link," adds Griggs. "The tolerance for foreignness is almost exotic. Practically all of the Americans in the financial district are guilty of the M.B.A. arrogance that there is a style that is the dominant style. Some of the perceived values are just white male values. White males in those positions should look at the written and unwritten rules in this particular professional discipline. You don't have to wear the same style clothes in order to sell stock; however, that is reinforced because most of the white males that have succeeded have succeeded by adopting that style."

Silicon Valley has had to adopt to diverse workforces. Many companies generate from 25 to 60 percent of their sales overseas. Asian immigrants make up high proportions of valley assembly workers and engineering talent can come from around the world. Griggs thinks the profit motive produces results faster than the legal arena.

"The companies are driven by different reasons," he adds. "There's the affirmative action driven firm like Xerox, that found once you've acted affirmatively, you've got a very diverse workforce and then you realize acting affirmatively isn't enough.

"Then you have companies like Hewlett-Packard which has been a global organization from day one and also ended up with a diverse workforce," says Griggs.

Yet, skeptics worry that companies printing business cards in both

FROM THE EDITORS OF ASPIRE

English and Japanese to match Far Eastern competitors and business partners may lose sight of Hispanics and African-Americans in the workplace, particularly at higher levels.

"I worry about the new labeling such as cultural diversity if it's a subterfuge for doing nothing, to show a few numbers and then rap about it," says Whaley.

"The internationalization of corporations will make it even more difficult for minorities to reach top levels," says Whaley. "If foreign executives and human resources organizations are involved, then there will be even less sensitivity to equal opportunity."

Whaley thinks it is important for minority groups to maintain pressure for full integration into society. "I'm not interested in equal treatment. I'm interested in equity."

"I'm still very much in favor of quotas and preferential treatment," adds Whaley. "Business runs on numerical goals. But minorities and women have been sold on the idea that it's a bad thing for them to get jobs because of affirmative action. It's a reverse psychology."

Whaley stresses, "I'm not saying that we should hire people if they're not qualified."

Griggs says the "competence" issue comes up often in his seminars. "I will not let people use the "competence" factor to derail this; otherwise that will give them a way out. If they force me to do that, I will remind them of all the white males who get jobs who don't deserve them. Often, the well-intentioned individual doesn't realize that they're picking people that they feel more comfortable with."

"Valuing Diversity" has been presented to a number of firms throughout the country as a film and as a seminar program, yet Griggs says he often finds the most resistance in Bay Area worksites.

"We in the Bay Area perceive ourselves to be the most liberal and open-minded people in the country, but our actual behavior does not always reflect that," he says. "We have probably gone further than anyone else with a live and let-live attitude, but there's no real contact. When you're working in an organization, it's not enough just to tolerate. The Bay Area seems to have stopped with its tolerance. I have found perhaps more resistance to discussing differences here than in some Midwestern areas."

Part Three
The Next Step

XVII
ENTREPRENEURSHIP

"Producers of goods are able to spin off and start your own company and produce goods."
                    Glenn Toney, Vice President-Human Resources, Applied Materials Inc.

Ed Dugger got a graphic lesson in the volatility of the financial marketplace on his way to address the Black Executive Forum.

From a pay phone in Chicago's O'Hare Airport, he learned that his next day appointment in Los Angeles had been cancelled. Drexel Burnham Lambert, one of the country's largest investment bankers and his destination, had gone bankrupt.

That incident underscores the importance of his venture capital fund's success during 18 years of focusing on financing minority entrepreneurs. For 15 years, Dugger has headed UNC Ventures in Boston, building it into a $30 million fund.

For UNC, times could not be better, because of the increasing supply of talented African-American executives poised to take over major companies.

"The next generation is well-educated, thoroughly trained, experienced, in mid-career and ambitious," the 6'4" venture capitalist told the Forum meeting at the Stanford Graduate School of Business. "They're feeling the pressure of the glass ceiling."

"They would rather build wealth and provide leadership, and say, "I will' instead of 'I'll ask'," he added during an hour-long talk and slide presentation.

He assured the audience "raising the capital is not the hardest piece" of diving into entrepreneurship. "Finding the right deal and assembling the team are critical. If you do those, you'll find money."

UNC provides risk capital, professional advice, access to its deal network and financing network for the three percent of entrepreneurs it chooses to fund. "We're emphasizing acquisitions because it affords managers an opportunity to start even with the eight-ball," said Dugger.

"We're often frustrated because we see deals, but don't have the right people to make the deals work," he adds. The fund has diversified into "deal banking" in which it makes an acquisition and then finds a management team to bring into the venture instead of waiting for an entrepreneur to come with the right package.

A current venture, Savat Enterprises, targets the funeral home industry, a lucrative business in which many established owners are selling out to large chains. "However, the black operators don't want to sell to white operations," he explained.

In the Bay Area, UNC is involved with area real estate investors in a $5 million real estate venture fund that is backing two projects in the Fillmore district of San Francisco and a project in the Napa wine country. Its first real estate venture resulted in the successful sale of a San Francisco medical office building. "We provide the front end financing which is the hardest for developers to get."

The average UNC investment is $1 million in syndication with several other funds for a total commitment of $3 to $5 million. "Our hurdle rate is 35 percent compounded annually. We want equity appreciation at that rate." For that investment, Dugger or associates would want to see a company that would reach a minimum of $20 million in sales during a five-year period.

"About 100 percent of the plans we get talk about why it's a good business opportunity," he quipped. "But they don't say why it's a good investment for us."

Dugger reminded the audience that a third of his investments will fail and another third will just barely make it. "The third that succeed have to carry all the rest," he pointed out.

SUCCESS SECRETS OF BLACK EXECUTIVES

In that risky environment, Dugger is clearly proud of having kept the fund on sound footing for 15 years. His success means something larger. "Our philosophical underpinning is that it is important for minority people, blacks in particular, to build a strong economic infrastructure that allows us to create and control wealth. We also want to see that talented minority executives have the same opportunity as anyone else to create businesses."

The reequipping of America's telephone system is a good sign to Fremont-based Atlantic Pacific Inc.

The company has built a strong business as an equipment assembler and distributor to telephone companies like Pacific Bell and AT&T.

Gary Evans, engineering manager, says, "There are a lot of new communities that need new phone service. All the old equipment that's out there needs to be renovated to handle the variety of new services that will be available over the phone."

Atlantic-Pacific is meeting those needs from three sites:

• an electrical manufacturing plant in Tracy which makes communications equipment and printed circuit boards from a 25,000 square foot facility with a staff of 30;

• a 30,000 square foot telecommunications distribution center in Livermore with 20 employees; and

• corporate offices in Fremont.

President Michael Clark founded the company to be an assembler and value-added reseller of telephone equipment to several of the regional Bell operating companies. Other clients include the Department of Defense and other government agencies and voice processing firms like Octel.

FROM THE EDITORS OF ASPIRE

Reference Sources for Entrepreneurs and Executives
Government Contracting Approaches
Business Planning

From The Editors of ASPIRE

XVIII
THE STAGES OF BLACK BUSINESS DEVELOPMENT

Because African-Americans have not had the access to the fundamental source of capital, land, our development of wealth has depended on cooperative ventures in which groups of people pool their resources, limited individually, but magnified by unity.

Although partially forced by necessity, this actually reflects an important cultural difference between European and African worldviews.

In the African civilizations of West and East Africa, property ownership was seen more as stewardship and many resources were considered property of the entire tribe or nation.

As educator/sociologist Annalee Walker points out in REACH WISELY: THE BLACK CULTURAL APPROACH TO EDUCATION, Black American culture is African spirit and thought carried out through European forms.

In the post-Revolutionary era, free Africans adopted the European forms of fraternal lodges, beneficial societies and churches to build their own culture with cross-linking boards managing these institutions, which met the social, cultural and welfare needs of the black community.

The black business community began the first of three stages.

Stage One, stretching from the 1600s to the Civil War, involves artisans and merchants developing small retail businesses during colonial times. Occupations like barbering, tailoring, blacksmithing and woodwork were areas where free Africans utilized their skills for themselves instead of for others.

Among the most notable successes of the colonial period was Paul Cuffee, the New England ship builder. These business leaders also took leadership roles in the lodges, churches and beneficial societies.

These institutions were the impetus for the second stage -- a great wave of business formation that swept the newly emancipated African-American community after the Civil War. These entrepreneurs now had a tremendous market because of the needs of the newly emancipated freedmen.

One of the first priorities was finance, which led to the creation of banks, savings and loan associations, credit unions and insurance companies.

The most stable and largest African-American financial institutions date back to that period. A look at two of them demonstrate ways that today's black entrepreneurs can create companies with staying power.

From The Editors of ASPIRE

IXX
MAGGIE L. WALKER
AND THE ORDER OF ST. LUKE

"We need a bank, a bank where our people can conduct their business with dignity."

Maggie L. Walker

Maggie Lena Walker was the first American woman to start a bank.

Considering that she lived in the former Capital of the Confederacy less than two decades after the War Between the States, that was a fantastic achievement.

However, the real testament to her legacy, in addition to the National Historic Site in her honor in downtown Richmond, Virginia, is that Consolidated Bank and Trust Co. is still in business 100 years later.

Vernard W. Henley, board chairman of the bank, still practices the same fundamentals that Mrs. Walker established for the bank. The result is one of the soundest banks in the country and a bank that, frankly, surprises most people when they learn that it is black owned.

Consolidated has been bashing stereotypes since the 19th century. Mrs. Walker was the head of the Order of St. Luke, a beneficial society founded in the 1860s that grew to have a national membership.

Constantly responsive to the needs of her members, Mrs. Walker perceived the need for a bank where they could handle financial transactions and have a safe, secure place to accumulate wealth.

Using the St. Luke membership as a base, Walker gathered a broad-based board from the Richmond area including church and business leadership and began a marketing campaign among the people of the city.

A stickler for detail, she imposed the strictest safeguards on the bank's assets to insure that not a penny of depositor funds would be lost.

For she knew, that her constituency could not afford to lose any of their hard-won earnings.

With the bank, Walker encouraged business growth in the Jackson Ward business district immediately around the bank and made home ownership possible for tens of thousands of black Richmond families through mortgages.

For most of the bank's history, it was the only source that African-Americans could turn to for business loans and home mortgages. The Main Street banks a few blocks away were interested in keeping the black population as dependent as possible.

The economic power of the bank gave the Richmond black community a different level of respect and clout than the community in most cities. It gave an independence that made contacts across Broad Street -- the dividing line between black and white in Richmond --encounters between relative equals. Rather than handouts, blacks sought access.

Walker was backed by Giles B. Jackson, a flamboyant Republican city councilman during the late 1880s, and John J. Mitchell, the fire-breathing editor of the Richmond Planet, from their Jackson Ward power base. The three had access to Presidents and governors.

But they remembered that their perceived power came from the nickles and dimes of the butlers, maids, carpenters and seamstresses who entrusted their resources to their leadership.

So they invested back into that community, with loans, mortgages, jobs, scholarships and donations.

They also fiercely insisted on standards of excellence in their business dealings that became important as role models for the students who admired them at the nearby Virginia Union University and Virginia State College (now University).

Generations of students knew that they could master accounting and finance because Consolidated Bank and Trust Co., or its neighbor, Southern Aid Life Insurance Company, served the needs of thousands of customers.

They also knew that they did not have to depend on Main Street to provide jobs for them. They could either work for the existing black-owned business community or begin their own businesses with the knowledge that they could find the financial backing.

For instance, young lawyers Oliver W. Hill and Samuel Tucker opened a practice in Jackson Ward in the 1940s. Shortly they became specialists in civil rights law, working in direct concert with the Virginia branch of the National Association for the Advancement of Colored People.

During the 1940s and 1950s, being a civil rights lawyer in Virginia was considered a subversive activity. Some activists were killed, and others had employment threatened.

However, the financial strength of Maggie L. Walker's creation allowed Hill & Tucker to fight for their clients secure in the knowledge that Main Street bankers could not tamper with their accounts or deny them access to credit.

When the U.S. Supreme Court heard the historic arguments in *Brown vs. Board of Education*, one of the cases combined for the purposes of the decision was a Prince Edward County, Virginia school desegregation case argued by Oliver Hill.

Twenty three years later, Hill stood proudly by as one of his partners, Henry Marsh, was sworn in as the first African-American mayor of Richmond.

Within a dozen more years, another black Richmond lawyer, L. Douglas Wilder, was sworn in as the first elected African-American governor of Virginia or any other American state.

They're examples of the multiplier effect of successful businesses and role models throughout a community.

However the progress of Richmond's black community during the past four decades has opened opportunities never envisioned before.

Now African-Americans can go to any bank, and see fellow African-Americans as tellers, loan officers and even vice presidents.

V.W. Henley, a graduate of Virginia State College, was one of those students setting their sights high because of the business giants of the late 19th century.

A year after Oliver Hill helped win *Brown vs. Board of Education*, Henley began working for Consolidated Bank and Trust Co., quickly rising to a post as cashier for the bank.

A subtle shift was taking place from the captive market Consolidated had built over the years to the wide-open competitive environment of retail banking.

Since 1955, Henley has not worked anywhere else but Consolidated, but he did not limit his universe to its four walls. He began aggressively participating in the American Bankers Association, attending the Stonier Graduate School of Banking at Cornell University, a gateway to the top echelons of American banking and sending promising executives from Consolidated.

Upon becoming Consolidated president, Henley saw that the bank had to modernize its facilities and procedures to compete in the free market economy.

He took the daring steps of constructing a new state-of-the-art main office, retaining an advertising agency to aggressively promote the bank, updating its logo and printed materials, and offering new financial products such as certificates of deposit and interest checking even before larger banks.

Using the slogan "Bring It Back Home," Consolidated sought to convince the newly prosperous black households of Richmond, now thoroughly infiltrated into area government, industry and health care jobs that the need to pool their resources to provide finance for the total community was just as great in the 20th century as it was in the 19th century.

The strategies have worked for Consolidated despite the opposition that one might expect from an entrenched set of stockholders and employees.

When black-owned banks in general have been declining in asset growth, Consolidated has grown to become one of the largest black-owned banks in the country.

Henley began expanding with two branches in Richmond and

acquired the Atlantic National Bank of Norfolk, creating a statewide bank.

"Essentially, when it comes to people's money, they are most concerned that it be safe and that they receive the service," says Henley. "They're not going to give us any loyalty as a black-owned bank unless we first meet those requirements. Once we do, then we can demonstrate why we can provide even better service than any other bank because we understand their needs."

It sounds like something from the mouth of Maggie Lena Walker.

FROM THE EDITORS OF ASPIRE

XX
C.C. SPAULDING
AND NORTH CAROLINA MUTUAL LIFE INSURANCE

"There is a wide range between the minimum requirements for holding a job and the maximum possibilities of that job. Any job or position will expand or shrink to the size of the person holding it."

Asa Spaulding Sr.

A similar message was being spoken by C.C. Spaulding of Durham, North Carolina, which came to be known as the "black business capital of America" early in the 20th century.

He created North Carolina Mutual Life Insurance Co., described by Ebony magazine as "the world's largest African-owned financial institution" with more than a billion dollars worth of life insurance in force a century after Spaulding began tramping up and down the country roads of North Carolina.

Spaulding understood the importance which the black community attached to a proper funeral and burial, another outgrowth of the African cultural worldview, and saw the need for a low-cost way of accumulating a burial reserve.

He priced his insurance so that even the neediest families could afford it and built a sales force that could collect the payments as small as five cents per week.

However, the creation of this extensive network was far more important than just providing insurance.

North Carolina Mutual Insurance agents became models of success who were visible in practically every home throughout most of the South. They took an interest in families, directing them to community resources in times of need short of death as well as being there for actual "homegoings." The N.C. Mutual branch manager in a

SUCCESS SECRETS OF BLACK EXECUTIVES

town was part of the black leadership of the city that helped to make decisions for such institutions as churches, hospitals and schools, and his sales force could quickly pass the word through the community on important issues..

Their concern for the people instead of just their money built a wide following that has continued for more than a century.

Like Consolidated Bank in Richmond, N.C. Mutual spawned a host of business ventures which led to Durham being christened "the black business capital of America." Mechanics and Farmers Bank, now stretching across North Carolina's Piedmont from Durham to Charlotte, was part of that business community, tied closely to North Carolina College, which fed a stream of new employee talent.

C.C. Spaulding's son, Asa T. Spaulding Sr., built on that foundation by bringing N.C. Mutual into the mainstream of the insurance industry's training and development.. A graduate of actuarial school, the younger Spaulding streamlined accounting practices and gave N.C. Mutual the ability to develop new insurance products to compete against the larger companies that began selling to black customers after the Civil Rights Movement.

His successor, William J. Kennedy, accelerated N.C. Mutual's ascent to the top rank of American insurance by obtaining corporate contracts to provide insurance benefits, and investing in such areas as broadcasting and venture capital.

Many of the black business ventures of the 1960s and 1970s had backing from North Carolina Mutual directly or through venture capital funds backed by N.C. Mutual like UNC Ventures of Boston, headed by Ed Dugger.

Kennedy also realized that insurance companies below a given size would not be able to compete in the overall marketplace so he began acquiring many of the smaller black-owned insurance companies to build even larger territories.

With more than a billion dollars behind him, Kennedy probably has more access to corporate America than any other African-American. As a board member, he has promoted increasing subcontracts with black businesses and been able to attract capital

FROM THE EDITORS OF ASPIRE

from white-owned companies to further leverage N.C. Mutual investments in black ventures.

Like Maggie Walker's bank, N.C. Mutual has found longevity and profitability in reinvesting black dollars in the black community.

XXI
MOVING INTO THE THIRD PHASE

Consolidated Bank and Trust Co., the nation's oldest black-owned bank, and North Carolina Mutual Life Insurance Co., the largest black-owned financial institutions, are perhaps the best examples, along with John Johnson's Johnson Publishing Co., of what it takes to create a successful black-owned business that not only is profitable but also undergirds the institutional base of our community.

They were forged out of a society that limited their customer base, but not their aspirations.

Yet they had an advantage over today's African-American businesses because they were confronted constantly with the extensive barriers erected to prevent their participation in the mainstream economy.

Therefore, those companies erected a structure that insulated them from those pressures and provided independence through dependence on their indigenous community. Because of that independence and the clout of a substantial customer base, far-sighted executives were able to eventually compete directly in the mainstream markets.

Less ambitious leaders of black-consumer businesses stuck to the tried-and-true markets which eroded under their feet.

To put it in perspective, Consolidated and N.C. Mutual thrived on the business from households with less than $1,000 per year in annual income, without property and without access to most well-paying professions in the country.

FROM THE EDITORS OF ASPIRE

They made their businesses an integral part of the community, but never took that community for granted. They kept standards high while constantly grooming new talent from the community to face new challenges.

One hundred years later, there are twice as many African-Americans as there were at the end of the 19th century. At least one million African-American households make more than $50,000 per year. One-fifth of the African-American civilian labor force holds professional and managerial jobs.

Despite a growing disparity with the white community, our progress during the 20th century is far beyond what our grandfathers and grandmothers could have envisioned.

In addition, the overt barriers to our entry into a number of industries have been reduced by the following factors:

• increased expertise in the black work force including scientific, management, and financial skills;

• governmental requirements to subcontract with "disadvantaged businesses;"

• the internationalization of markets, both business-to-business and consumer;

• the impact of technology on the cost of entry into large markets.

So, with a vastly more affluent market and reduced barriers, the opportunities to become the Maggie Walkers, C.C. Spauldings, Madame C.J. Walkers and John Johnsons of the future are tremendous.

As we have moved into the third stage of black business development in America, a tremendous obstacle has emerged along with the increased education, income and access -- the cult of individualism and the belief that "you can't trust a brother."

As a result, we have seen the rise of hundreds of individual African-American entertainers and athletes who individually earn more than the total African-American business community did nationally in 1890.

Although the success of the Walkers, Spauldings and Johnsons was multiplied from pennies and nickles and dimes, the millions now

flowing through those hands have not produced the same multiplier effect in today's black community.

The tragedy is that those dollars could go even further in the hands of some of the emerging managerial, technological and marketing stars our community has produced.

The barrier that the black business pioneers of the 19th century did not overcome was that of creating large industrial enterprises that could employ the great mass of our people. That was strenuously opposed.

The volume of inventions that came from African-Americans during the "age of discovery" at the turn of the century ranging from the golf tee to the electric stop light to shoe-making machinery. Yet, unlike Edison's Bell System or General Electric, those inventors did not get to reap the fruits of their inventions.

Even Sears, Roebuck & Co., founded in part by an African-American who came up with the idea for an inexpensive mass market catalog, passed out of his hands before it became a national icon. Even still, his creation helped educate millions because new owner Julius Rosenwald endowed hundreds of elementary and secondary schools throughout the South.

The missing ingredient was financing, the capital needed for research and development, marketing and tooling up for mass market manufacturing. The financial barons took control of the discoveries because of their control of capital and distribution systems.

Today's generation of innovators still faces the same lack of access to capital markets. Although untested Steve Wozniak and Steven Jobs could get $3 million to launch Apple Computer from their garage, Roy Clay, an African-American who developed Hewlett-Packard's first computers in the mid-1960s, could not get venture capital to start a similar business.

Howard Smith's ability to raise venture capital still points out how many other African-American entrepreneurs have been unable to launch large companies although they've had superior products.

Frustration fills many entrepreneurs who look at the increasing wealth of the African-American community, and the individual wealth of some celebrities and wonder why can't we put our money together.

We can, and we have.

That's where the lessons of the last century can propel us into the future.

In order to attract the support of the larger black community, new enterprises must demonstrate a commitment to that community through jobs, advancement potential, role modeling for our children and support for its institutions. Those enterprises must be an integral part of the community.

The "computer nerd" model of Silicon Valley does not fit in with our communalistic culture. Being lost in one's work is a recipe for being lost.

Part of the networking that needs to occur is a linkage between the entertainment/athletic community and the business/professional community.

It should happen in a structured fashion that eliminates opportunities for rip-offs and unmet expectations. No one entertainer/athlete, be they Bill Cosby or Michael Jackson or Michael Jordan, should be made to feel that they "owe" any one. The fruits of their successes are theirs.

However, an ongoing organization of African-American athletes and entertainers, the kind that comes together on an ad hoc basis for specific events and causes, could provide a channel for reinvestment in the black community.

To make this organization most useful to its members, it could also take on some of the advocacy that black actors and athletes need in their dealings with large entertainment organizations, including referrals to professional providers. It could work with large national advertisers to expand endorsement opportunities.

Such an organization could work in concert with the national civil rights organizations and national African-American professional groups to identify the most promising business opportunities that would foster the economic development of the African-American community. These groups could screen out the hustlers and celebrity-seekers.

Like the business networks that emerged in the 19th century, this ongoing network could work behind the scenes to create changes in American society from a position of strength, not protest.

In the third phase of black business development, which we date from the mid-1960s, the most dominant changes have been the linkage for the first time with government and large corporations and the sheer growth in numbers of black businesses.

Black involvement in the industrialization of America in the 20th century dates back to the turn of the century when labor recruiters encouraged the migration from the tenant farms of the South into the factories of the North and Midwest.

Black labor was used as a counterweight to the white labor movement, which originally kept blacks from its membership. The development of the Congress of Industrial Organizations and its merger with the American Federation of Labor led to the integration of black unions such as A. Philip Randolph's Brotherhood of Sleeping Car Porters into the broader labor movement and membership for blacks in such unions as the United Auto Workers.

The movement represented by Randolph and other black labor leaders became a pressure point for forcing corporate America and the government to broaden economic opportunities for African-Americans..

During the New Deal, it meant inclusion of Negroes in the job creation programs of the Works Progress Administration, Civilian Conservation Corps, etc. As World War II sucked in the United States, the black labor movement accumulated enough leverage to insist on the first Presidential Executive Order, by President Franklin D. Roosevelt in 1944, banning discrimination in war industries.

That began a gradual evolution of federal policy from encouraging fair employment to also encouraging fair business opportunities. President Richard M. Nixon was the first chief executive in 1969 to explicitly advocate "black capitalism", launching the Office of Minority Business Enterprise with a mandate to boost government procurement and provide training and financing to minority-owned business.

The increase in African-American legislative power generated by the Voting Rights Act of 1965 took that ball and ran with it. Rep. Parren Mitchell, D-Maryland, a product of Baltimore's black business and political community, made minority business development his specialty in Congress as the Congressional Black Caucus grew from two members in the 1960s to more than 20. Mitchell began inserting amendments encouraging set-aside programs for disadvantaged businesses into most federal appropriations, most notably defense procurement and transportation.

Secretary of Transportation William T. Coleman, who served under the administration of Gerald Ford, gave administrative force to Mitchell's legislative efforts, creating several offices to encourage minority participation in mass transit, rail, highway and airway construction projects.

Between the transportation and defense provisions that mandated plans for subcontracting significant amounts to minority and small business, it meant practically every major corporation in the country now had a specific need to contract with minorities.

At the local levels, where African-Americans rose into executive leadership positions such as mayors and city managers, even more dramatic steps could be taken.

Some cities, such as Richmond, Virginia, adopted goals of 30 per cent procurement with minority businesses for city contracting. Atlanta became famous for its ability through both legal goals and quiet behind-the-scenes negotiating to wring major benefits for black businesses in the construction and operation of the massive Hartsfield International Airport.

The success of these efforts brought a backlash, even more dramatic than the backlash for such programs as school desegregation. Whereas it became unfashionable to directly oppose integration (hence the code word *busing*), the opposition to minority procurement goals has been unstinting. The Associated General

Success Secrets of Black Executives

Contractors of America and its local affiliates carried a number of court cases culminating in a late 1980s Supreme Court ruling that threw a number of local business affirmative action plans into jeopardy.

The Court did not touch federal minority procurement laws and regulations, ruling that Congress had the right to impose such guidelines.

However, a hostile attitude to affirmative action and regulation in general during the 1980s under the Reagan and Bush administrations has lessened the pressure on corporations to meet federal mandates regarding contracting with "disadvantaged small businesses."

That attitude and a decision by the Reagan administration to "graduate" companies from the 8(a) program of the Small Business Administration made it tougher for companies to leverage federal contracts into substantial businesses.

Section 8(a) allowed government agencies to select certain contracts for award only to small businesses certified under section 8 (a). In response to complaints that some companies existed only to bid for 8(a) contracts, a time limit and a revenue limit was placed on participation.

Minority businesses complained that their dependence on government work was more a function of racism in private businesses than their own choice.

Even these setbacks have not slowed the third wave of black business growth. Government intervention opened the doors to business formation, but it took real skill in business to survive and grow. Those skills have taken most black businesses even further than any government program could.

According to the U.S. Census, the receipts of black-owned businesses grew from $9.6 billion in 1982 to $19.7 billion in 1987-- a growth of 105.5 per cent. Government spending with black businesses barely topped $2 billion in the latter year.

In that same five year period, the actual number of black-owned businesses grew to 424,165, a 37.6 per cent increase over the 308,260 recorded in 1982.

FROM THE EDITORS OF ASPIRE

Between 1980 and 1990, the black population of the U.S. grew from 26.5 million to 30 million, a gain of 13.2 per cent. So black business formation is growing far faster than the growth in population.

Also, that growth is coming in new industries. Black-owned retail outlets, including barber shops, beauty shops and grocery stores declined 6 per cent from 70,811 to 66, 229.

The number of black-owned financial, insurance and real estate firms rose 108 percent from 12,957 to 26,989.

Those figures are now five years old.

We can expect the 1992 Census of Minority Business to show similar jumps.

Impact Resources of Columbus, Ohio tracks the minority population extensively. It showed a 50 percent increase in the number of black households nationally with more than 50,000 income from 1989 to 1991 from 700,000 to more than 1 million. That kind of income growth did not likely come from employment.

XXII
THE FOURTH STAGE

At each stage of black business growth, African-American entrepreneurs have adjusted to the opportunities made available by the larger society.

The continuum of progress spirals upward. In the mid-50s, it was a significant coup for Nat King Cole to have a variety show on a major network.

In the 1990s, it is expected that an Arsenio Hall be his own executive producer for his variety show.

Likewise, it was a major breakthrough in the 1950s when Chuck Cooper became the first black player in the National Basketball Association.

In the late 1980s, black entrepreneurs bought the Denver Nuggets franchise.

Moves like those mark the beginning of the fourth stage of black business in America.

Since the end of World War II, African-Americans have fought to demonstrate that they could compete when given an equal opportunity, and also, that they could successfully market to the general audience.

The Nat King Cole syndrome, in which some southern network affiliates refused to carry his show for fear of adverse white reaction, seems far off.

Now, African-Americans are among the most recognizable celebrity spokespersons for major consumer products. Entertainers are no longer relegated solely to "race" music or art. Their talents are seen around the world. Black women even won Miss America two years in a row.

FROM THE EDITORS OF ASPIRE

Twenty years earlier, those kind of symbols would have been enough. But an increasing sophistication about markets and finance means that even the teen rap stars off the corner know the advantages of being their own producers.

The racial barriers between markets have, ironically, been broken down by white-owned companies. Looking closely at the demographics of America's population, they have gone into the markets once left to ethnic companies such as hair care and cosmetics.

Revlon, Estee Lauder and Alberto Culver all have invested major sums into personal grooming products for African-Americans -- targeting the one major consumer manufacturing field dominated by black companies.

Food manufacturers, soft drink companies, fast food restaurants and athletic shoe companies have all found vast rewards from marketing to ethnic communities. As a bonus, they have found that slogans developed for ethnic markets, and celebrities geared to those markets, often work even better in the general marketplace.

For instance, "We Do Chicken Right" was a slogan originally developed for the African-American market by a black-owned agency that became the icon for Kentucky Fried Chicken nationwide.

The colors and patterns popularized by "world music" artists such as Bob Marley and Fela Anikopu Kuti festered in the streets of cities like New York and London and took hold of the world of fashion. Now, African prints are almost required in high fashion designs.

Athletic shoes were an industry that relied on dueling sets of scientific research until African-American superstars led a quadrupling of the industry. Can you imagine Nike Inc. without Michael Jordan, or Bo Jackson?

A shibboleth of advertising has been demolished. African-American spokespersons do not turn off mass audiences, and they appear to be even more effective in building product awareness and loyalty.

During the 1991 Super Bowl, PepsiCo relied on pianist Ray Charles and three gorgeous backup singers to imprint "You've Got

Success Secrets of Black Executives

the Right One, Baby" on the American consciousness.

In a recessionary economy, the fastest growing segments of the American consumer market appear to be those highly influenced by Afro-centric marketing, either with celebrities, music or styles.

We've taken a slightly circuitous route to make the following point. American and worldwide consumers are highly influenced by the culture and symbols of African-Americans--a trait that has been worth billions to corporate America.

Major corporations have done the test marketing that demonstrates that the time is fast approaching for a fourth stage of black business that does not set its goals at being a subcontractor or supplier to a bigger company or the government.

Instead, these fourth stage companies will take the cultural assets of the African diaspora to create products with mass appeal. How can this happen, one might ask, given the lack of access to capital and distribution networks that have traditionally hampered African-American businesses?

First, we must demystify how large multinational enterprises get launched in the late 20th century. Nike Inc. is a good example. The company is basically a marketing engine.

Its advertising creates consumer demand, based on the image of athletic superiority fostered by its celebrity endorsers. The shoes themselves get made in Taiwan, by a plant that also makes the brands for several other athletic shoe makers.

Any of us could order a set of custom-made athletic shoes just as easy as Nike. For that matter, we could order a custom-made automobile designed to our specifications.

Once we had our product made, then we would need to hire a sales force. Well, no. There are thousands of manufacturers representative firms specializing in every imaginable industry who can market your product into the correct retail channels.

So, manufacturing and sales a re covered. What about product development and research? You could keep that in house, but you could just as easily hire a university professor and several graduate students in your particular specialty to conduct the research you need. Once again, you don't have to make an upfront investment in laboratory space or staffing.

In fact, for any function you might imagine for a large corporation, there are companies that will provide that service, often on a commission basis.

Management guru Tom Peters once told an audience that a study of a $4 billion British corporation discovered that every job in the company could be subcontracted out except the chief executive officer and a fax machine.

In the 1990s, ideas can become wealth thanks to the support structures that undergird American businesses. Racism is no longer as important because you may never see your business partner face-to-face. A telephone line and a computer modem can be your complete interface. Whatever your race, if the money is flowing, a deal can be made.

Fourth stage black businesses have broken the psychological slavery of thinking that they must prove themselves to a larger company in order to be accepted.

Their self-esteem comes from their acceptance in the marketplace. Many unsuccessful companies failed because they failed to have faith in their business, seeking a wealthy suitor to undergird their efforts. The same amount of attention paid to the business itself would have yielded far more than the amount available through outside sources.

That acceptance in the marketplace comes as a result of the success secrets we laid out in the beginning chapters of this book.

Howard Smith's Clarity, David Brown's GBI Communications or Rick Harris' Preferred Office Systems are perfect examples of fourth stage companies. They have the following characteristics.

- Championship Spirit -- Each company has set out to be the best in the world in their chosen industry and has structured the business to make that happen.

- Endurance -- The staying power to overcome business downturns and reverses and the patience to wait for opportunities to unfold.

SUCCESS SECRETS OF BLACK EXECUTIVES

• Mastery -- a command of the technology to create and operate their product and a willingness to stay on the leading edge of that technology.

• Commitment to Service --the ability to provide service is a factor that separates survivors from losers in the business marketplace.

• The Special Touch -- either in service or in product, one factor which no one else can provide and that customers are willing to pay a premium price to have.

FROM THE EDITORS OF ASPIRE

XXII
FOURTH STAGE OPPORTUNITIES

"Fifty percent of the Fortune 500 disappeared between 1980 and 1989."

Tom Peters, management guru

The dominant factor driving world markets during the last few years of the 20th century and the 21st century will be freedom.

Technological advances and increased access to knowledge have made it impossible to keep people chained to large structures and old orthodoxies.

When the Iron Curtain fell, followed in short order by the Eastern European puppets of the Soviet Union and then the Soviet Union itself, it was a crisis of confidence in the old Communist order.

Apartheid is falling in South Africa, far slower than anyone would like, but likewise as a function of a n ideology which could not stand the light of the truth.

A similar change is occurring in the world economy, dominated for several hundred years by the mercantile interests of London and New York.

For that period, those interests have kept a tight rein on the means and resources of production worldwide through their trading markets. For instance, most commodities sold by African nations have to go through London or Paris or Brussels because the communications links go back to the former colonial powers.

Politically around the world, mass movements have overtaken politicians because the masses learned that they could speak directly for themselves instead of being bartered around by politicians.

Economically, anyone with a modem and a fax can do business

internationally whether they have a seat on the London Mercantile Exchange or not.

For consumers, the power of knowledge will empower them with far more choices than they've ever had before.

Most products will become smaller, lighter and smarter with more custom features.

Rather than a Calvin Klein original, the 21st century consumer will be able to diagram their own creation on a computer, imprint it with their own signature and proudly wear it within hours.

Interactive television already exists. Rather than wait for a writer's script to unfold, the viewer can decide how the story will proceed and end, based on the viewer's decisions.

Stereo television, that allows viewers to decide which language they want to listen in, already exists.

Notebook computers with more processing power than the original roomsize Univac computer already are a hot consumer item.

Let's look at a fourth stage company that is riding the wave of freedom around the world.

Riding a wave is a good analogy for Ronald Lee Jones, the founder and chief executive officer of Colossal Graphics Inc. of Palo Alto, California.

As a young man, he liked to ride the waves off Monterey along the Pacific Coast. Once he frightened his grandmother by getting knocked out while surfing.

She made him promise not to surf again.

Another youthful promise to his grandmother stuck with Jones. A blood infection brought the teenager near death. As he lay in a hospital bed for several months, his grandmother charged him with this statement. "You've never reached your potential. When you get up from here, I want you to realize your potential."

Jones made it up from the sick bed, defying the odds, a characteristic he has made into a personal trademark.

SUCCESS SECRETS OF BLACK EXECUTIVES

FROM THE EDITORS OF ASPIRE

Less than two decades later, Jones strode to the headtable of the Interracial Council for Business Opportunity annual dinner in New York to receive the award for Minority Entrepreneur of the Year for his creation of Colossal Graphics Inc.

Let's trace how Jones got to that stage. After high school, he took a job as a technician with Hewlett-Packard Co. Naturally dexterious with machinery, he began looking into the insides of the computers he serviced.

Along with a group of other engineers, he started a company to write programs for the early generation of personal computers. That venture did not work, so he went on to other Silicon Valley technical jobs. However, his personal need to explore the limits of his technical creativity went unfulfilled.

When the software and hardware emerged to allow desktop publishing, Jones noticed that the same approach could be used to take images from personal computers to print on a large four-color computer plotter.

Plotters, developed for the military to print out maps and reconnaissance photos from satellites, had previously required the power of a mainframe computer to process the amount of information required to create the four-color print.

Jones and his associates created mathematical algorithms to compress the data and invented a raster image processor (RIP) to convert the personal computer files into a format that could be output by the plotter.

That meant any image that could be created on a personal computer screen could be printed in full-color as large as 42 inches wide and 12 feet long.

Usually prints that large had to printed in volume to be cost effective. With Jones' invention, the computer

SUCCESS SECRETS OF BLACK EXECUTIVES

user could print as few as one copy.

At that point, Jones began to run into the kind of obstacles that have bedeviled black inventors throughout American history.

He had received $250,000 in venture capital from the Presbyterian Economic Development Corporation, an arm of the United Presbyterian Church, U.S.A. to finance his early research and development.

To fully exploit the discoveries, he would need much more capital. The venture capital barons of Silicon Valley were unwilling to put money into his venture, despite Colossal's having produced a working model and having attracted a seed round of financing, usually the most difficult to achieve.

Even more trouble came on the horizon. The leading plotter manufacturer, a subsidiary of Xerox, refused to cooperate with Colossal's efforts. Jones says, "They looked at what we had and figured that if someone black could do it, their engineers could do it themselves, but they were never able to do it."

The company even refused to service Jones' own plotter because of the modifications Colossal made. "Their position was that their market was to work with engineering workstations, period." The wrangle ended in a legal settlement that barred Jones from receiving service or supplies from the Xerox company.

Cash got tight and Jones was forced to leave his own apartment to sleep in the office next to his plotters for several months. "I had to go to the public tennis courts every morning to shower," recalls Jones.

Yet he never lost the image of his grandmother looking over his sick bed, challenging him to reach his potential. Jones wouldn't give up.

Software companies would not work with him, thinking his product was too esoteric for the general market.

Jones was determined to make his company into the Eastman Kodak of large-format color printing. So he used his biggest weapon -- his product.

He began bombarding potential clients with three-foot by four-foot Colossal Grams, created to look like telegrams.. System sales began trickling in.

Paul Koze, owner of a San Francisco blue print service bureau, saw the potential application of the Colossal technology for his customers. He bought a system, then a second one and convinced members of the Reprocad Network, a national alliance of blue printers who shared files over a computer network, to purchase a volume of Colossal workstations and software.

That meant a substantial boost in sales of Xerox plotters. Still the company would not enter into an OEM (Original Equipment Manufacturer) agreement with Colossal to allow Jones to sell the plotters directly as part of a total system.

Never a small thinker, Jones began promoting his product on an even larger scale. When major league baseball went on strike in 1989, Jones, an avid San Francisco Giants fan, wound up losing his deposit on a trip to spring training.

He began a campaign called "O.U.C.H - Only Unrepresented Consumers Hurt" using his Colossal prints to get signatures from irate fans about the loss of the national pastime. The campaign continued even after the games started.

Although some associates thought he had lost his mind, Jones was crazy like a fox. What he was doing was gaining valuable free publicity for his product.

Meanwhile, Reprocad Network members began using the product, receiving rave reviews from customers who were able to generate posters on demand, just like desktop publishing.

They began a joint marketing campaign for the service including advertising and trade show booths. At one of those booths, an Englishman learned about the service.

Before returning home, he flew out to Palo Alto to meet with Jones, not only wishing to buy a system, but to represent Colossal for European sales.

Soon, Colossal Graphics Limited was opening in London, with Xerox Engineering Services - Europe as its partner, selling Xerox plotters through Colossal.

"It's ironic," muses Jones. "While the parent company wouldn't do business with me that one of their foreign subsidiaries 5,000 miles away would, and we're only 30 miles apart."

Another Colossal campaign began with the Persian Gulf War. Jones began traveling from college football bowl game to professional game around the country, gaining signatures from teams like the Pittsburg Steelers and Philadelphia Eagles and the Air Force Academy on messages directed to the troops in the field.

As a result, American Express Co. and Lockheed used Colossal prints to send best wishes to some of their employees serving in the reserves during the war, and Jones wound up on the CBS Evening News with his product.

Once again, a slightly hare-brained scheme brought in new customers.

The most Colossal promotion took place at the Minnesota Metrodome. Jones obtained the permission of state and local officials to set a Guinness Book world record for the largest computer generated print by rolling out a giant Colossal print, segmented into 1200

FROM THE EDITORS OF ASPIRE

panels across the playing surface where the Super Bowl XXVI was about to be played. He got 3M to contribute tape to attach the panels, Specialty Toner to contribute the ink and Graphics Technology International to supply the paper. DHL Worldwide Express, official carrier for the National Football League, brought the one ton shipment from the Bay Area to Minneapolis.

With determination and verve, Jones has overcome the lack of capitol and has carried out product development, international marketing and national promotional campaigns.

He has overcome one critical psychological hurdle. He is never afraid to ask.

"My problem is that I turn some people off because I'm in their face," Jones notes.

He relies on mentors like Howard Smith and Ken Coleman to keep him in touch with the outside world and to bounce his ideas. They remind him to maintain a focus on profitability, cash flow and strategic positioning.

As the company grows, Jones has begun bringing in savvy African-American executives to handle sales and financial functions.

The obstacles are still daunting, but this kid who got his start in Watts is looking to make a big impression on Silicon Valley.

In the process, he wants to provide opportunities for kids like himself. Eventually, Jones wants to mass produce his own plotters and he has a site in mind, an abandoned school in East Palo Alto, a predominantly black community in the shadow of upscale Palo Alto and Stanford University.

Jones' goal is to not only train African-American youth in technology but also to outfit the facility with a world-class velodrome and other facilities to be used

SUCCESS SECRETS OF BLACK EXECUTIVES

for sports camps.
   It's a big vision, but most folks have learned not to discount Ron Jones.

   Fourth stage companies are companies who use savvy and skill to overcome the lack of capital. Eventually, the Ron Jones of the world will break through into the world marketplace, where they can bypass the rigid financial elites of America.
   Can one small business make an impact?
   Take the example of Spike Lee, a film student at New York University, who scraped together a black and white film using friends called *"She's Gotta Have It"* in the early 1980s.
   Rejected by major studios, Lee took his film to the market. He created a cult following and now can command $28 million budgets from major studios.
   Lee also reshaped an industry. From his lonely example, in 1991, 18 African-American filmmakers directed full-length feature films. Some, like cinematographer Ernest Dickerson and actor Bill Duke, got a boost from working with Lee.
   Others got the opportunity to make films because Lee had shown that films with an Afro-centric theme could attract general audiences.
   Racism is still evident in the treatment of these filmmakers. Their budgets and promotional efforts are a fraction of those awarded to untried and even failing white producers.
   But each advance moves the body of African-American filmmaking further along a path for which there is no turning back.
   The increase in programming is important for another reason.
   Access to the airwaves is expanding.
   During the past 10 years, the Federal Communications Commission has conducted one of the greatest lotteries in history. The FCC has created new bandwidth opportunities in the frequency spectrum.
   The new spaces have gone to such services as cellular phones,

FROM THE EDITORS OF ASPIRE

nationwide paging, interactive television, and wireless cable. Each award has been through a lottery. That means Mr. Average Joe has the same opportunity as Metromedia or Viacom, if they know about it.

Ken Jackson, an engineering graduate of San Jose State University, found out about it shortly after finishing college and has never had to work for anyone except himself.

"When these lotteries come up, they are usually distributed based on local areas," says Jackson. "To qualify, all you have to do is submit an engineering study of the area, which you can get for $500. For the most desirable cities, hundreds or thousands apply. To maximize their chances, partnerships are formed among the bidders. If anyone in the partnership has their number chosen, they share it with the remainder of the group. Your stake in the partnership depends on how much you put in."

Jackson began playing this lottery when cable television franchises were being awarded. His first investment of $500 netted him $50,000 in cash.

"The big players usually don't compete in the lottery," says Jackson. "They just wait until a winner is picked and then they make an offer."

"If you're chosen, you have three choices -- sell immediately, build a system yourself or enter a management contract with another company to build it for you," adds Jackson.

He has been part of winning partnerships for several cable systems, cellular phone franchises and nationwide paging. He is building a cable system in Alabama.

The future is being decided in these lotteries, contends Jackson. In the same way that some sporting events and entertainment have moved to cable television, increasingly the access to information will be on a for-pay basis through these esoteric new services.

Within five years, it will no longer take expensive new wiring to conduct these services into American homes. Local telephone companies are installing ISDN wiring instead of the traditional twisted pair lines. ISDN is a protocol that allows the transmission of tremendous amounts of data including television signals through phone lines.

The reason that African-American filmmakers have had such a difficult time getting in movie theatres and on television is that African-Americans have not controlled the means of transmission of the films.

Thanks to the FCC lotteries, there is a potential to at least take a share in the ownership of the new networks. With a concerted cooperative effort, African-Americans can play a dominant role.

Jackson says, "Come on in, the water's fine."

FROM THE EDITORS OF ASPIRE

XXIII
FOURTH STAGE OPPORTUNITIES
THE GREAT FIRE SALE

The largest redistribution of wealth in world history is occurring as you read these pages. Unfortunately, much of it is flowing back into the hands of those who had it in the first place.

The Resolution Trust Corp. has $500 billion in assets of defunct savings and loans to get rid of. It acquired the property by taking over those institutions and foreclosing on their bad loans. Ironically, most of those S&Ls had horrible records of lending to black homeowners, despite the notion that blacks are bad credit risks.. Somehow, their good credit risks took 'em to the cleaners.

But it's no time to gloat.

RTC was established to dispose of all that commercial real estate, residential subdivision land, cars, furniture, art, jewelry and whatever harebrained assets the S&Ls squandered money on.

If you have 29 cents to get a stamp, use it to get on the mailing list for your nearby RTC regional office. If just buying a house is your goal, then RTC properties are placed on auction regularly. Auction prices tend to run much lower than regular prices. If you're really poor, that's great. The law that created RTC, thanks to the Congressional Black Caucus, gives a preference to low-income residents and non-profit groups serving them in the allocation of RTC housing.

If going into real estate development is your cup of tea, then you can combine with a group and bid on a whole subdivision, once again at a fraction of the market price.

Success Secrets of Black Executives

The bulk of the American populace has glazed over at the news of the S&L debacle. They must have, because there would be a revolution if most people realized the scope of the ripoff of their taxpayer dollars by the securities markets.

The money made by the speculators who lured the savings and loans into risky investments and loans still exists, hidden from the reach of federal regulators.

That means you and I get left holding the bag for covering the deposits insured by the "full faith and credit" of the United States government.

However, that same speculator money has been following the RTC auctions religiously, and has the opportunity to repurchase what they should have lost.

The actual purchases of the savings banks themselves have definitely followed that pattern. Most bank acquisitions have been by players in the financial markets, including banks wanting to expand across state lines.

Anyone can get on the list of potential bank purchasers, but coming up with the capital to run a $2 billion asset bank is another question.

Once again, there is a way to do it.

Jim Buie, a bank manager in Los Altos, California, is advocating use of the National Consumer Cooperative Bank by potential bank purchasers. The NCCB was created during the Carter administration and practically forgotten about during the last dozen years of Republican administrations.

But it still has millions of dollars from Congress to help launch consumer cooperatives. A cooperative is any organization of consumers who band together to purchase something in volume. Examples include rural electric cooperatives or farm cooperatives.

In many urban areas, cooperatives run grocery and clothing stores. Credit unions are also examples of cooperative businesses run by their members.

Buie developed the concept of a cooperative forming for the purpose of acquiring thrift institutions from the RTC . Members would have the benefits of receiving credit cards, loans, insurance and other benefits through the savings bank.

With just 100 members, the cooperative can receive start-up funding, professional advice and training from the NCCB.

The merger mania among the large banks also provides an additional opportunity. Each merger must be approved based in part on the institutions' performance under the Community Reinvestment Act (CRA), a mid-1970s law designed to force banks to make loans in areas previously "red-lined" because of high proportions of minority residents or businesses. Most banks' records stink.

Despite the CRA signs in most bank lobbies, very few people know that it matters whether the bank gave them a loan or not and why they got turned down.

A 1991 study by the federal government shows that African-Americans of similar income and characteristics got turned down for loans by American banks three time s more often than white Americans.

It appears obvious that the even-larger banks will have even fewer incentives to obey the law. These "healthier" conglomerate banks now require the kind of credit to open a checking account that it once took to hold a gold credit card.

That has resulted in a massive income transfer out of minority communities in the form of check-cashing stores, which charge a fee to do what banks do for free.

Those same low-income persons whose taxes underwrite the deposit insurance that keeps the banks open don't get the service from the banks. However, a substantial income is being made from them by check cashers who can not provide the additional savings and other services that banks provide.

That presents a market niche for a new kind of bank, built on a combination of defunct S&Ls and spun-off branches of merger banks, which often fall in the heart of minority communities.

Rather than make public assistance recipients wait in humiliating lines at the first of the month, it would arrange direct deposit with state and federal governments and issue them automated teller cards with which they could shop at their leisure with pride. But they could also learn budgeting skills by keeping their funds in a safe place.

This kind of bank would carry out the same practices as Maggie Walker in the 1800s. Rather than tying up a customer with credit for a car loan, it would establish savings accounts that allow the client to save up for desired purchases. With a proper balance, they could either pay cash for it or then borrow the amount at favorable terms, and still have the interest from their savings.

American bankers have pushed a healthy chunk of the population out of the banking system, and all they have to show for it is a record of failure and fraud. It's time to reclaim banks for the purposes they were intended for -- to serve the mass populace with financial services -- and not as playthings for speculators.

HOSPITALITY

My old dean at the Howard University School of Communications, Tony Brown, has been advocating that we "Buy Freedom" for more than a decade. Perhaps his greatest suggestion is that all black organizations cancel their conventions for a year and use the money to build a single black-owned convention facility.

The black travel and tourism budget in America amounts to more than $2 billion yearly. If you were paying attention earlier, that's the same amount that the federal government spends with black-owned business.

Has the light come on yet?

Once again, it is a question of rising expectations. Black Americans have been so happy just to be able to get a hotel room in this country, and then to be able to afford a hotel room, that we are just getting to the point of owning the hotel.

The National Baptist Convention, U.S.A., the world's largest black organization with 7 million members, went more than 100 years without a national headquarters until Dr. T.J. Jemison pulled its 5,000 churches into a campaign to build the World Baptist Center in Nashville. That was just several years ago. Now they can have their meetings in their own facility.

In 1992, the monument to the Buffalo Soldier will be enshrined at Fort Leavenworth in the museum to blacks in the military.

I submit that we should go even further, because people don't go to a hotel or a convention center. They go to a place.

As African-Americans, we need to create our own place. I'll call it "The Mother Land" for the sake of discussion. Like the National Baptist Convention headquarters and the new National Civil Rights Museum at the old Hotel Lorraine in Memphis, it should be in Tennessee, which is a central location close to the great bulk of the black population, which would save on travel costs.

A Tennessee site would allow more than 60 per cent of the nation's black population to be within a day's drive of the location.

We should buy some land owned by black families since the 19th century and create an African Disneyland, complete with African-themed rides.

But unlike the Marine World Africas and the Busch Gardens -- the Dark Continent, this theme park would celebrate the people as well as the animals.

It would include historical exhibits and geneological files so that families could actually trace their roots. They would be tributes to black music, perhaps even holographic images of great black stars in nightclub settings, so one could relive the Savoy. There would be lots of black talent dancing, singing and performing on numerous stages..

The park would also feature exhibits from the black populations around the world. Most blacks do not know that the Ganges River in India is named for a conquering black general or than the last king of Hawaii was black or that Napoleon had 12 black generals serving under him in the Napoleonic Wars.

A special sports section would store memorabilia from such greats as Arthur Ashe, Muhammad Ali and Wilt Chamberlain. There

Success Secrets of Black Executives

should also be state-of-the-arts sports training facilities where today's stars would conduct year-round seminars for visiting young and adults. Since a sizable number of brothers and sisters golf, a championship course should be laid out just for them.

With all that going on, it would be hard to keep many people focused in a convention. That would not be much different from today's conventions. There should also be a facility for a meeting hall and exhibit space.

If this seems outlandish, consider what one television preacher was able to do in Heritage Land U.S.A. near Charlotte, N.C. Jim Bakker went to jail for abusing his parishioners trust, but that does not detract from the soundness of his basic concept.

On $2 billion per year, we could sustain that kind of facility and perhaps a similar one on the West Coast. Other expansion could take place in Brazil, South Africa and even Europe.

Black people are capable of just as much imagination as Walt Disney.

EDUCATION

The biggest problem that black parents face today, more pressing than drugs or gangs, are the public schools.

It is inconceivable to blacks who grew up in one-room schoolhouses and ghetto schools to witness their children with all the advantages fail in today's suburban educational centers.

Most parents are just frustrated, but an increasing number are realizing that it is not the child, but the school that is the source of the problem.

In the continuum of rising expectations, once we were happy to attend a school, then to attend any public school. Now we insist on being educated, and educated to compete with anyone.

The current public schools will not accomplish that with their ethnocentric focus that denies the accomplishments of African-American historical figures and black children in the classroom today.

There will be a fantastic market for educational materials and even private schools for African-American children. The growing tide of racism in America and the frustration that all parents feel with the schools will lead to the adoption of tuition vouchers.

Although most civil rights organizations oppose tuition vouchers, vouchers would actually solve the problem that school desegregation was intended to ameliorate.

Black schools worked fine as educational institutions and transmitters of culture. They just didn't have equal access to resources.

If every kid in America got the same amount of money for his school, it would create enough of a pool in most urban areas to underwrite effective Afro-centric education.

Most parents, if given a choice between the cultural genocide happening in public schools and quality black schools, would choose the latter.

CUISINE

Have you ever noticed that every nationality has its own restaurants in America but black people? Just look in the Yellow Pages, where there are perhaps one or two listings under "Soul Food" compared to dozens of Mexican or Chinese restaurants.

We're not referring to the scattered rib joints and barbecue shacks, but either fancy restaurants or large chains featuring black cuisine to go.

Black children asked to bring their native dish to schools have been known to bring bags of burgers from McDonald's.

Like the singer said in "Soldier's Story," "It's a low-down, dirty shame."

In the third wave, it was an honor to see Bill Cosby hawking "Puddin Pops" or Michael Jordan's picture on a box of Wheaties.

Fourth wave companies will make distinctive products that go straight to the supermarket shelves.

Should those shelves be owned by Korean grocers? They will if

SUCCESS SECRETS OF BLACK EXECUTIVES

African-Americans fail to seize the opportunities presented by grocery chains who have preceded the banks and retailers in a flight from minority community.

Fourth wave companies should operate major grocery chains, buying from cooperatives of black farmers. Can we do this? Does the name George Washington Carver ring a bell. Without him there would have been no Skippy peanut butter.

Carver was unselfish enough not to enforce his patents. He perhaps realized that they would have been taken from him anyway in the "robber baron" days.

However, there is still extensive agricultural research going on at historically-black land grant colleges and Carver's own Tuskegee Institute. So the seeds of future products are perhaps sitting in those labs.

Hundreds of African-Americans have held jobs as product and brand managers for Kellogg's, General Foods, Coca-Cola, PepsiCo, Phillip Morris, R.JR Nabisco and Proctor and Gamble.

Thousands of African-Americans hold retail franchises throughout the fast food industry.

Even larger number have served as store and department managers in grocery stores.

Detroit Lions running back Barry Sanders, the quietest superstar in sports, speaks loudly with his money. In his first year as a professional football player, he returned to his hometown in Oklahoma and opened a supermarket because there was none in his community.

He deserves a lot more respect than all the athletic shoe endorsers in the world. If every African-American superstar of his stature would start at least one retail outlet of some kind in their home town community, it would make a powerful statement about our personal commitment to our people. No athlete or entertainer makes it without the love and support of a broader community. Those people who had a stake in that talent can also reap the rewards instead of seeing the star pass by in their luxury car.

I n the second phase, black dollars were multiplied. In the fourth phase, those dollars can achieve geometric progression.

From a selfish viewpoint, African-Americans spent $22.4 billion yearly on groceries in 1990, according to the Statistical Abstract of the United States.

By channeling a fourth of that sum into our own community, we could solve much of our unemployment crisis..

In the third stage, we march to protest Korean grocers who shoot African-American teens.

In the fourth stage, we open our own supermarkets instead of liquor stores and stock the stores with products produced by African-American companies. In the same way that Julius Erving and Magic Johnson have popularized owning a beverage distributor, Barry Sanders will popularize opening grocery stores. The new stores can be serviced through a wholesaling cooperative that would also produce products designed for African-American palates. As Tom Goss said earlier, it is a winning formula to appeal to those tastes.

The trucks from that cooperative can stop at African-American fast food restaurants.

And instead of getting mad, we'll get smart. We'll invite Asian-Americans to invest in the supermarkets rather than having to run them themselves.

APPAREL

It's enough to make you shake your head. A teen-aged rap star rearranges a floppy hat into distinctive shape for a performance. Soon every kid in town has to have one of those hats.

It's great for the hat maker, usually in Taipei or Hong Kong. But Kangol has not created one job in the 'hood.

Fashion is one of the quickest routes to merchandising success in American business. It begins with a concept - a basic human need that these clothes are intended to fulfill.

Everything after that is execution. The same cutting shops shape the fabric, the same sewers compile it and the same buyers look over the finished product at the fashion expositions.

Most American fashion concepts arise out of urban

neighborhoods. If traced back far enough, they arise from some African-American kid whose clothes were too big, or belt too tight and their creative way of making it look like they intended it that way.

One of the fastest growing African-American retail businesses are boutiques, often an outgrowth of hair salons. The styles they're creating are on the leading edge of American fashion, but blocked from mass markets by exclusionary practices of major department stores.

Generally, these stores bring a high degree of skill and talent but have yet to develop the marketing savvy to reach broad markets. Once again, the cooperative approach to business can begin to propel those stores into their rightful share of the $15.6 billion spent by African-American consumers on clothes. Rather than each store spending meager amounts on advertising and marketing, they should advertise together.

Money being spent on programs, combined can generate radio and television buys that reach a greater audience.

Combined fashion shows can generate revenue and bring attention to the entire group of stores. Cooperative marketing works for malls, it should work for African-Americans in fashion as well.

That can be extended on a regional and national level to create national campaigns, perhaps using African-American celebrities, to stress the quality they provide and to feature the designs of emerging talents.

The continuum of progress proceeds from the success of African-American hair care concerns and their support of hair salons. Now, savvy entrepreneurs in the personal care market see new profits in catering to the total man and woman.

In the third phase, the black business community has managed to hold on to its stake in the personal grooming market.

In the fourth phase, we can project some of those national grooming products companies expanding into apparel using their distribution and retail power. It is a move that will protect them against competition in their main lines from larger companies.

FROM THE EDITORS OF ASPIRE

Otherwise, they will find their niches growing smaller and smaller as the market grows bigger and bigger.

TECHNOLOGY

Black inventors have played a major role in American commerce. However in the first, second and third phases, they generally did not reap the fruits of their inventions.

The 21st century presents a wide open playing field for their imagination.

American industrial might is crumbling before the onslaught of Japanese and European innovation. Most American companies are downsizing and cutting back basic research and development. The role of defense spending on American technology has never been more evident than now, when the military spending boom fueled a massive surge in computing power.

In several of the key fields for the future, African-American scientists and engineers hold the leadership roles on the cutting edge. Marc Hanna's Geometry Engine still outperforms any comparable integrated circuit.

Dr. David Brown's voice mail system makes current systems seem like a Model T.

John Moon's disk drive systems have allowed Apple computers to grow smaller with much more power.

Howard Smith's Clarity Rapport will be the standard among horizontal software for workstations.

There are other African-American technical geniuses with even more far-sighted and earthshaking technologies in areas as diverse as holography and lithium storage batteries.

"Quiet as it is kept, black engineers are ready to take over technology the same way we took over athletics," says Colossal Graphics' Ron L. Jones. "The four top semiconductor designers in Silicon Valley are black. If you took black athletes away, America would not be competitive in the Olympic Games. Without the contributions of black technical people, we won't be able to compete internationally in business."

As Jones points out from his own example, black culture emphasizes practicality and utility. "We see things differently and that's why we're apt to come up with innovations."

The only real handicap to a black technical renaissance is a prevailing attitude throughout the country that African-Americans, whose ancestors created the most widely used numerical system, can't handle mathematics and science.

"We need to project our scientific superstars the same way that the Michael Jordans and Bo Jacksons are presented to our young people," says Jones, who has waged a lonely battle with major mass media including 60 Minutes to run stories on black technical achievements as opposed to black drug abuse and gang violence.

"If black kids could see the Mercedes and BMW's that black engineers drive, and the houses they are able to afford, without having to worry about whether they'll get cut from a team or whether the next album will sell, they'll understand that it is a much more achievable dream than becoming the next Michael Jordan," says Jones, who grew up as a youth in Los Angeles' Watts area.

"Becoming a music or athletic superstar depends so much on luck," he notes. "For everyone who makes it, there are twenty-five more with the same amount of talent who don't get discovered."

"But if you graduate with a degree in engineering or computer sciences or chemistry, you have almost a 100 per cent chance of achieving your goals," adds Jones. "There are many more jobs available, and once you have technical skills, you can always create your own job."

The world of the 21st century will be dramatically different than the one we faced in the 20th century. The following development will drive the direction of technology.

- A massive increase in computing power. The invention of the integrated circuit in the mid-1950s made today's computers possible. An integrated circuit consists of a set of pathways etched on a silicon or galium arsenide chip that serve as highways for the flow of electrons. Electricity is created by the free flow of electrons attracted off of atoms (remember the wool test from science class or getting shocked by your rug). The narrower the channels for those electrons, the more highways can be created on a single chip, leaving room for more memory and for more instructions.

Currently, integrated circuit makers are just reaching the one micron (one millionth of a meter) width for those highways, which many considered the limit of how thinly those passageways could be etched, using current methods. The significance of Dr. Joe Gordon's work for IBM Corp. is that he is leading toward methods of building chips one electron at a time. Rather than etching out a highway, the chip can be built to include them as narrow as possible.

Today's computers use one megabyte integrated circuits. The megabyte is a measurement of the memory the chip can process. Four megabyte chips are already in commercial production. Sixteen megabyte chips have been tested experimentally.

At the four megabyte level, the contents of a current 486 computer can be contained in single chip. At the sixteen megabyte level, one could walk around with the power of a mainframe computer in a wristwatch.

Every electrical product in our society will have to be redesigned over the next three decades, with features we can scarcely imagine.

Your shower head can be programmed to deliver water at the exact temperature you want.

Your kitchen chair can be automatically programmed to adjust to your weight, height and desired posture.

Your car will never get lost as it consults a navigation satellite to determine the proper direction and optimum route.

You will be able to communicate with your children whereever they are using a microphone no smaller than a button, attached to their clothes.

There is no limit to the new products that can be created using

Success Secrets of Black Executives

that expanded computing power. Most of them will not be created by the existing electronics conglomerates.

Tom Peters points out that 50 per cent of the Fortune 500 disappeared from 1980 to 1988 through acquisitions, mergers and/or bankruptcies.

Large industrial enterprises on the Henry Ford scale find it difficult to adjust rapidly enough to absorb and recreate new technologies. The retooling and retraining necessary takes years.

In the 21st century, small will be better.

Anyone with an idea can retain a product designer, go to a modeling shop, develop a prototype and attract production capital or enough advance orders.

Should the black workers being laid off from the General Motors plants in Detroit meekly consent to finding jobs flipping hamburgers?

They don't have to.

African-Americans are noted as automobile enthusiasts, particularly with custom designs for their cars.

A black-owned California company, Motorsport Auto of Santa Clara, has developed a thriving business customizing luxury cars like Porsches and Mercedes, including those of many celebrities in the Bay Area. Owner Reggie White started as a body shop and then began adding his own distinctive touches.

In the fourth stage, there are opportunities to build custom cars on a mass level. With the latest technology, robots like those from Joe Avery's Adept Technologies Inc. can change manufacturing patterns for each individual car.

The vision of a Reggie White can be fed into a computer aided manufacturing circuit and reproduced as often as orders demand.

The Big Three will be dinosaurs in the 21st century. It is a trend that has already occurred in the steel industry. Giants like U.S. Steel failed to see the handwriting on the wall and smaller steel mills, with more advanced technologies, overtook them.

Increased computing power is a great leveller. No large industry will be sacrosanct, because bigness will no longer be an advantage.

FROM THE EDITORS OF ASPIRE

The customized products we're been storing in our garages and workshops can now be brought to market.

2. Advances in bioengineering.

Carey Bolden and Jim Knight have witnessed a revolution in biotechnology during their three decades in the business. Now chemists consider themselves bioengineers, because they're no longer just making discoveries about the nature of the human body, but they're aggressively moving around the pieces of the puzzle.

Most of those discoveries have not yet reached the health care market yet, although bioengineered antibodies and epidural drug delivery systems have already come into use.

The approach to treating disease will change to one of managing health.

Solving the massive health problems of the black community will be an opportunity for tremendous profits because the major pharmaceutical firms have very little interest in those issues. Most of the health care system is in full flight away from inner-city neighborhoods.

The base of African-American health care specialists must combine with people like Ron Williams of Blue Cross of California, Bolden and Knight to begin designing solutions to those problems and bringing them to market.

Dr. Ernest Bates of San Francisco is a prime example. The physician perceived a need for hospitals to have expensive equipment that they simply couldn't afford. He created American Shared Hospital Services Inc. to buy and operate the X-ray machines and magnetic resonance imagers for the hospitals, plus provide such services as security and laundry more effectively than the hospitals could on their own.

A hidden resource is the rich body of medical knowledge from Africa and South America and even the United States drawn from folk and herbal remedies.

For instance, Kenyan doctors say they have found a cure for the

SUCCESS SECRETS OF BLACK EXECUTIVES

Acquired Immune Deficiency Syndrome. This announcement has been ignored and/or attacked by the worldwide medical establishment. If it is true, then America's black community, out of self-defense should bring this treatment to this country. With a former dean of Morehouse's Medical School as secretary of Health and Human Services and the attention generated by Magic Johnson's announcement that he is HIV-positive, there is no greater opportunity to force attention to finding a cure to this health scourge in our community.

The increased interest in the history of Egyptian civilization will also yield many medical discoveries. The Egyptians reportedly carried out advanced brain surgery 5,000 years ago.

For those who would say that bioengineering is beyond the capabilities of the black community, let us think of Dr. Daniel Hale Williams, the Chicago black doctor who performed the first open heart surgery mere months after Emancipation, or Dr. Charles Drew, who discovered blood plasma, making blood banks possible, or pioneering biochemist Dr. Percy Julian, given his own laboratory by major drug companies in the early 20th century to create powerful treatments.

3. Lifestyle changes

The global village is becoming a reality, yet at the same time, producing a renewed emphasis on one's own culture. We're seeing simultaneously, worldwide communications access, and the breakup of modern nation-states that cross cultural borders.

African-Americans are well-equipped to compete in that environment because of a legacy of being cross-cultural in order to survive in the United States of America.

Many foreigners have tremendous misconceptions about African-Americans because of a lack of direct contact and a reliance on Hollywood for their images of blackness. African-Americans likewise have misconceptions about foreign lands based on the distortions we've heard.

FROM THE EDITORS OF ASPIRE

African-Americans who have leapt across those barriers to become international have been rewarded handsomely. It would have been inconceivable for the U.S. government to put Muhammad Ali in jail over charges of draft evasion. He was the most recognizable man in the world at the time and the international blot on the American image would have been devastating.

Even, domestically, the lines that keep Americans of different flavors and colors separated by neighborhoods and cultures are coming down.

It means a tremendous opportunity for crossover products, which have a base in one ethnic group and then become available to the mass population.

No longer will it be necessary to make a product successful to the entire U.S. market. The subcultures can carry it through h the development stages. It also means that effective marketers will create more than one version of their product -- not only a Hispanic version, but a Puerto Rican style, an El Salvadorean, a Mexican style -- to maximize their markets.

In the 21st century, consumers will have an explosion of choices. The closer one can get to their unique, specific desires, the better off one will be and that's an advantage for the new entrepreneur over the large company.

IVXX

Blueprint for a Fourth-Stage Black Business

"This is the best time in history for African-Americans to go into business. At the beginning of this century, you needed massive amounts of capital to launch an industry. Now all you need is a telephone, a fax and a product to sell."
   Tony Brown, founder Buy Freedom campaign

The first ingredient for a successful fourth-stage African-American business venture is the development of a team, consisting of:

- an attorney;
- an accountant;
- an experienced sales manager;
- a product development specialist (engineer or other discipline depending on the product);
- a graphic designer or marketing communications specialist.
- founder/chief executive/visionary.

Normally, the founder will fall into one or more of the other categories. Cooperation is critical, but it takes a visionary spirit to actually carry the concept through to fruition. The founder has to be the one person who takes the long-range view of what is best for the business.

FROM THE EDITORS OF ASPIRE

Team development can begin while the members are still in other jobs. Either the founder or the product development person will be the first required to make a full-time commitment.

For most purposes, the business should be organized as a corporation authorized to issue several million shares of stock. Team members can apportion founders stock in relationship to their investments of money and/or services.

After initial meetings, the business goal should be distilled into a three page document called a "concept paper." This approach was developed by the Silicon Valley Entrepreneurs Club, an organization of more than 300 team-driven startups that extensively studied business formation.

The concept paper should include:

(1) The proposed company name
(2) A one-paragraph description of the company's goals
(3) A one-paragraph description of the company's product(s)
(4) The unfair advantage that your company has over any other company (product, personnel, service, etc.)
(5) A listing of the progress that the team has accomplished
(6) The company's needs (investment, expertise, contacts, research)
(7) A response form

This document is ready to be sent to potential backers of the business ranging from vendors to customers to investors. Distilling down the essence of the business to no more than two and one-half pages also helps to focus the enterprise. It is important to have all the various facets represented.

The response form gives recipients blanks to say what kind of help they can provide, and their reaction to the concept presented.

Most entrepreneurs do not get this kind of feedback, and it is usually available for free. The concept paper list should include industry sources, trade associations, bankers, venture capitalists and associates of the team members.

Success Secrets of Black Executives

Expect perhaps a two to three percent response. From those response, you can begin building an advisory board that can give continuing feedback and legitimacy to the company.

From the feedback, the team should gain a sense of how the idea will be received in the marketplace. Advisory board members may also suggest ways to gain advance contracts for the product and low-cost ways to have it manufactured.

After that exercise, it is time to think seriously about capitalizing the business. A well-heeled team can expect to invest $250,000 at a minimum to get any substantial business off the ground. Members can provide the seed capital themselves, the shortest route. After gaining feedback from advisory board members, the team members can have more confidence in the validity of their concept.

That kind of financial commitment will make outside investment a smoother process in the future. There are a variety of ways to leverage the value of funds invested to minimize risk. We recommend against second mortgage loans to start a business. That equity should be a fallback position in case the business does not work.

Team members can place an initial amount of $25,000 to $50,000 in a cash management account available through most stock brokerages. These accounts constantly invest funds, provide business credit cards and margin loans for a percentage of the value invested.

This resource can continue growing and build a record of cash flow for the business.

If the team members do not have the resources to fully fund product development, the next strategy is to develop an intermediate business plan that markets the expertise assembled in the team. This could include consulting contracts and other subcontracts. This provides an additional opportunity for team members to learn how to work with each other or whether they can at all.

One idea is to develop a newsletter and seminar business on the product. This provides an opportunity to gather information and to develop a reputation as an expert on the product.

From The Editors of ASPIRE

A second is to serve as a broker for the commodities required to make the product, building relationships with the essential suppliers needed. Get on the bid list for federal and state agencies which can provide initial contracts.

If enough cash flow can be generated to pay ongoing expenses, then the initial capital can be allowed to grow

Both of those ideas provide opportunities for the essential function for a new business, networking. Each team member should have a goal of 20 new contacts per month, targeting essential constituencies needed for the growth of the company.

A primary source of contacts should be organizations of purchasing agents. Buy a membership for your financial person in the area chapter of the National Association for Purchasing Management. Attend every meeting. If your product fits a business-to-business niche, this will be your primary market.

If you have a retail consumer product, you want to become a feature in the area Retail Merchants Association.

The local Black Chamber of Commerce and emerging Black Executive groups, plus organizations like the National Black MBAs and the National Society of Black Engineers can help identify potential supporters/foes within major companies and potential team members.

If there is a nearby association of entrepreneurs, fit them into your schedule. Entrepreneurs as a group provide a tremendous energy and the vitality of having figured out practically every way to do something without any money. You'll gain much more than the price of admission each time you attend.

So you're six months down the road and the product is ready for market. It is time for a comprehensive business plan. It is important to wait several months before compiling this document. Many of the original assumptions outlined in the concept paper will prove to be incorrect.

Psychologically, it is easier to adjust from a short concept paper than from a 200-page business plan.

If you want to have a good laugh, do a business plan at the

beginning and then come back and look at it six months later.

Completion of a business plan means that your firm is poised for full operation. The reality of being an African-American business in America is that the normal one-in-one thousand chance of getting major venture capital is increased by a factor of at least one hundred.

That won't change much until there are more African-American controlled venture funds.

So we proceed on the assumption that you will not be able to attract sizable equity capital before the start of production.

There are other ways to capitalize your business that will result in the founders keeping a much larger share of it.

• Distribution contracts -- either wholesalers or sales rep firms can commit to purchasing a guaranteed number of the products. If you have established credibility through your interim business, perhaps they will pay in advance. However, you can finance the purchase orders either through a bank or through factors. Some factors will issue a letter of credit to a manufacturer guaranteeing payment once the goods are finished and shipped. With that kind of guarantee, you can get most products made.

• favorable credit terms -- find a supplier who has excess capacity or inventory and ask for 90 day terms. If you have good personal credit, you can convince the supplier to carry you with a guarantee of continued business.

• licensing -- a hot product can attract firms who will produce it in return for the right to manufacture and market it. Depending on the capital cost to produce it, you may consider licensing it in return for royalties. An alternate approach is to license the foreign rights.

However, your best strategy to maintain control of the product and the proceeds is to use added value pricing. Design the product using very inexpensive raw materials. Add value through your design. Your price can then yield a markup that capitalizes the business through sales.

Your pricing strategy should keep the cost of materials and production at no more than 20 per cent of the sales cost. Another 40 to 50 percent will typically go into overhead and sales. If you can't

FROM THE EDITORS OF ASPIRE

make a 40 percent net operating income, you're doing something wrong and will probably wind up in bankruptcy court.

Let's say you've decided to market a coffee maker with a radio-clock alarm that automatically begins brewing at the right time of the morning or day and supplies the desired station right on the button.

You purchase coffee makers through a Taiwanese supplier for $1.50 apiece in bulk. At your facility, you install the clock-radio feature, using components that cost $1.25.

So for less than $5,000, you have enough inventory to create 2,000 products.

Check out similar products in stores. They might sell for $19.95, but they don't have your unfair advantage. So you can add a premium of 50 percent or $29.95.

Your cost of materials is $2.75. You can afford another $2 in labor to make it. Retailers will want at least a 40 percent markup and your sales cost will be 10 percent.

That's how money gets made in America. Buy low and sell high.

With your $20,000 profit from selling 2,000 products, you can then invest in making another 8,000. You also have a base of customers that you can use in advertising.

White-owned companies have the luxury of dropping several million in advance promotional advertising before product launch. You probably won't.

Fortunately, word-of-mouth is even more effective. Prepare releases for trade publications, using testimonials from satisfied customers and retailers.

Once you break the trade press, which can take several months, then you're in position to utilize the general circulation media. Most general circulation journalists are ignorant of business, including those working on business desks. They rely on the trade press to check the validity of new products.

Don't forget the black press, which is hungry for stories about black success. They'll give you more weight if you break in with the trade press, first.

Success Secrets of Black Executives

To break into the general circulation media, you'll need a promotional gimmick that qualifies as a legitimate news story.

Oakland, California entrepreneur Cheryl Munson, named the Governor's Entrepreneur of the Year for her Cousin Mattie's Daddy's Sister's People line of greeting cards and novelties, had all the ingredients of a fourth stage business going for her, when she rode the wave of Santa Claus in 1990.

She opened a "Very Merry Black Christmas Store" just after the Thanksgiving holiday. Newspapers and radio clambered over the story to deal with the paucity of Afro-centric gifts for Christmas. Munson not only turned a profit on the two-month adventure in retailing, but also received carry-over business for her catalogue business..

Ron Jones, whose Colossal Graphics Inc. has made the outrageous commonplace, also rode the Christmas spirit by cooperating with a California police department to produce a life-size mounted replica of a police officer to place in retail stores to deter shoplifting.

His Clone-A-Cops aired all over the nation in December 1991.

Neither business had to spend a dime on advertising.

The next step is to propel that publicity into actual sales. Make copies of articles, and begin fax marketing into the distribution channels you need to access. Line up enough advance orders to go into full production.

If you decide to market your clock/radio coffee-maker through department stores, organize a tour to visit the locations.

Once you don't need it, then investors will come crawling out of the woodwork. However, then you're in position to negotiate on the most favorable terms.

Then, you can offer preferred stock, guaranteeing a certain level of return for the investment, without giving up the voting stock in the company. That is the best approach to retain control of your dream and to maximize the capital gains for the original founders.

With that investment, you can then begin to judiciously advertise, beginning once again with the industry press, to test themes. Put more of your consumer budget into promotions and premiums because these are more measurable.

The results from these data provide valuable insights for where the product's best markets are.

In the original concept plan, you should have projected which additional l products would come from the original concept. With cash in hand, you can begin a schedule that unveils new products and product lines at least once per year.

A couple years later, you're ready for an initial public offering, in which your shares are traded on public markets.

Then, the founders and investors get to cash out handsomely or accumulate wealth from the growth in the value of their stock.

Early on, a compensation plan should be developed that fairly apportions those benefits among the founding team. Elements should include sales commissions, bonuses, stock options and whole life insurance. The plan should be developed with future employees in mind, including non-executive staff.

This is an important way to exercise the multiplier effect. One of the ways that Silicon Valley grew so quickly was that employees of the start-up companies were able to accumulate wealth in addition to salaries from their stock options.

They could then afford to launch their own companies after gaining expertise working for the original start-up. This is something to encourage rather than discourage. It is one thing to protect the value of your intellectual property. However, there are far more benefits from having a slew of companies owned by proteges in the marketplace.

Hopefully, fourth stage black businesspeople will learn from the example of their political counterparts. The high tide of black electoral success is likely to fade because many black officeholders refuse to allow new blood into their seats.

Because of the lack of advancement opportunities for those officeholders, they stay in the seats until they die or are beaten by non-black opponents.

As a community, we lose.

Long-lasting, progressive companies like North Carolina Mutual and Consolidated Bank and Trust Co. have thrived because they've both had advancement opportunities and succession plans within, but they've also supported staffers who go into other business ventures.

Being insecure is part of the game when you're black and in business. However, it is important to recognize the line between constructive fear, leading to patience and wisdom, and paranoia.

FROM THE EDITORS OF ASPIRE

XXV
OVERCOMING MENTAL SLAVERY

"The impulse to dream has been slowly beaten out of us by life. "
Les Brown, motivational speaker

As Abraham Lincoln often said, he did not wage the Civil War to end slavery. He sought to keep the Union together.

The Emancipation Proclamation kept the country together by removing the slave labor base that undergirded the Confederate war effort.

Less than two decades later, the same justification--keeping the Union together--was used for the Compromise of 1877 that essentially allowed the South to reenslave the black population.

America has never had a commitment to full opportunities for its black citizens. Each wave of progress has occurred because of the convergence of the black freedom struggle and the larger society's need for black labor. We've been this country's economic Rapid Deployment Force.

The actual chains have been removed, but the psychological chains are even more burdensome.

African-Americans, as a group of people, exhibit all the tendencies of co-dependency.

We have low self esteem.
We engage in fantasies to hide our real pain.
We don't trust ourselves or each other.
We don't place a priority on our own progress.
We instead place highest priority on helping other people (usually of other ethnic groups).

SUCCESS SECRETS OF BLACK EXECUTIVES

    Co-dependency is a defense mechanism in the mind that seeks to protect the body from the effect of intense, searing psychological pain -- in this case, the constant, debilitating pressure of racism.
    The only way to overcome this tendency is to, in the words of San Francisco minister Cecil Williams, face the pain.
    It is akin to taking an aspirin for a headache. It covers the pain, but you never realize what is actually causing the headache until a brain aneurism bursts and takes your life.
    That's what our group and individual codependency does. It kills us inside. It affects our families, our relationships, our friendships and our careers. Its symptoms can range from drug and alcohol abuse to sexual promiscuity. It also results in a "rip-off" mentality that we project on to each other as a sign of the lack of self-respect.
    As our rap artists remind us, a woman is something to conquered and used, rather than loved and honored, and vice versa. That leads to an expectation that we will be "ripped-off" which can become a self-fulfilling prophecy.
    Today's slavemasters have taken hold of these tendencies to keep us under the ball and chain.
    The big picture is right in front of us, but our blood-covered glasses impair our vision.
    Slave mental attitudes extend to the way we perceive African-American-owned businesses.
    We expect them to not offer superior service and products and we don't regard their owners with much respect. We don't invest in them, and more often than not, we don't even buy from them, even when they're more convenient.
    Instead, consumer surveys show that we are the most loyal customers of the major department stores, even when they're charging us twice as much.
    The percentage of blacks owning German luxury cars indexes at twice the percentage in the general population, despite there not being a single African-American BMW or Mercedes dealership, and no significant advertising by either in African-American media.
    We are just happy to have the fantasy of success, rather than the

real thing.

Getting the real thing hurts.

And the average African-American is already saddled with more hurt than they can absorb.

Let's look at some of the typical events that can occur in the life of an upwardly mobile African-American male in the 1990s. Keep in mind that this is a *success model*.

TWENTY-FIVE YEARS IN THE LIFE OF AN AVERAGE AFRICAN-AMERICAN MALE WHO ACHIEVES SUCCESS

In **kindergarten**, a teacher slips and calls his "Little Black Sambo." His parents raise Holy Hell and the teacher apologizes, but is not fired.

By the **second grade**, another teacher tells him that he's not good in math. The parents have him tested and he scores three grade levels above the norm.

At **age ten**, he's been told by his first storekeeper to get out of his store because he happened to go in with a group of buddies.

Before reaching the **age of puberty**, he is likely to have had his first encounter with local police -- something like this.

> Riding his bike down the street, two police cars come out of nowhere, surround him and toss him across the hood of a car. They then interrogate him about a burglary (heaven help if they're looking for a rape suspect) and may actually take him in. The parents show up and get him out, but the odds are very likely that he could pick up a police record right then.

However, back in school, coaches have seen his athletic prowess and insist that he try out for a sport.

"Can I play quarterback," he asks.

FROM THE EDITORS OF ASPIRE

"No, you'd be better at running back," comes the reply.

In his **high school** classes, teachers steer him into the least challenging subjects and while he's actively competing, he can pass with little effort. His parents remind him to study hard, but do not use the lever of banning him from sports because of the lack of other alternatives. Both working, they're concerned about all the other things he could be involved in.

Fortunately, he meets a former athletic hero from that same school of ten years earlier. He's now working as the janitor at the school. The janitor pulls him aside in the hallway of the shower room after football practice.
"Son, I just wanted to let you take a look at the future unless you get your priorities in order. You remember when I was the all-state running back back when you were a little bitty kid."
"Yea, I wanted to be just like you."
"That's what I'm trying to prevent."
"I let the cheers of the crowd seduce me into thinking everyone loved me and that my future was secure. All I had to do was just score more touchdowns."
"You know, when I've got the ball in my hands, I feel like I'm free as a bird."
"But you're not. You're not calling the shots. You can't even get the ball unless they decide to hand it off to you. I didn't realize that until I got to State University and suddenly I became a fourth-string defensive back. I got disillusioned, my grades fell, I got a girl pregnant and started smoking crack to deal with the pressure."
"Damn."
"That might not happen to you. But for every

SUCCESS SECRETS OF BLACK EXECUTIVES

Herschel Walker and Barry Sanders, there are 25 brothers like me. We toted that barrel and lifted that barge until they didn't need us any more and now we're just hangin' on. Look at me, my teeth are rotted out and I look like I'm 50 years old. My son won't listen to me, because his mom has turned him against me. But maybe I can reach you, because you remember what I used to be, and you see that's where you are right now. You've got a choice. Do you want to end up like me or like my friend Phil, who played second-string linebacker?"

"Who's he?"

"You know the doctor with the big office on 10th Street and all the pretty nurses."

"Yeah."

"I get tickled every time I go by there. He gives me free checkups once a year. When Phil was in high school, he couldn't find a girl and whenever we wanted to go out and hang on the corner, he would say I've got to study; the white man makes it hard enough, I don't want to help him"

"So you're telling me to hit the books."

"I'm saying a lot more than that. Phil tells me often how full of b.s. those books were. I say, I knew that. That's why I didn't pick 'em up. But what he found was that if he learned how to find out things, he could find the real truth for himself. Phil never started on our high school football team, but he got an academic scholarship to State University. He was going through a lot of the same kind of changes I was going through, with everybody acting like you didn't belong there. But Phil was used to it, because he never fit in anywhere. He just hunkered down and studied harder because he had a goal to prove them wrong and took biochemistry, the hardest subject

there. They put him through so much shit there and in med school, but I've got to give it to the brother. He hung in there."

"You know, I'd like to meet this doctor and maybe he can give me some advice about choosing a college. I think I can go anywhere I want, but I don't know what I want to do. I guess you're right, I might not make it to the pros and even if, I do, I'll need something to fall back on afterwards."

The janitor's face fills with tears and he warmly embraces the young football star. "Man, I watch these kids come through here every year and they get the same game run on them. You're the first one to listen to me. Come on, let's get in the car and I'll take you down to Phil's office."

The doctor advises him to enroll in the area Consortium for Minorities in Engineering, which offers an after-school program with tutoring in math and science and career exploration in engineering fields.

He does and uses his football scholarship to study engineering. He plays for four years, starting some, but not becoming a big star. Most importantly to his parents, who still wonder what happened to him in the eleventh grade that caused him to become studious, he graduates with a bachelors of science in engineering.

Still bitten with the football bug, he tries out for a pro team, but doesn't make the cut. He goes back to the janitor and the doctor to ask for advice. They suggest that he go to school for another year to earn a Masters in Business Administration.

With their encouragement, he applies, is accepted and receives a cooperative learning job with a technology company that brings him some income.

The president is an alumnus of State University and welcomes him warmly. The combination of school and work is challenging, but there is a problem. In both environments, people always ask him

SUCCESS SECRETS OF BLACK EXECUTIVES

about football, but never about the actual work to be done. He overhears several of his classmates talking one day.

> "This case study is kicking my butt. I never knew business school would be this hard. I wish I was one of those affirmative action students like (mentioning his name) and didn't have to study so hard."
> "Yeah, they don't belong here anyway. They can't run anything, just look at all those countries in Africa."

He might as well have been shot in the heart. These were his study group partners, and they were just bigots.

He couldn't focus for several days, until he went to visit a black faculty member on the staff of the business school and recounted what he had overheard.

The professor shook his head.

"They never change, do they? Well, I just want you to know better. That's the one thing we can change."

The professor takes him to a meeting of the African Engineering Society on campus, where 20 graduate and undergraduate students go over their school projects and their dreams for their countries. They encourage him to go to see the continent for himself.

He feels better. Leaving the meeting, he's charged up and decides to go over to his office at the company to work on a project. It's after ten p.m. when he enters the building through a back door.

> Walking down the hallway, he feels something cold against his neck. Then he hears a voice, "Stop your black ass right there, buddy. Raise your hands."
> He stops, raises his hands and begins to say, **"I wo...."**
> "Shut up, before I kick your stealing ass..."
> The security guard pulls his hands down and handcuffs him. Then the guard whirls him around.
> There's a flash of recognition. The guard sees the

155

company badge in his pocket.

"*I was telling you I work here.*"

"Oh, sorry, we have to protect our security here and I'm not used to seeing your kind here this late at night."

"**I want your name, because I'm going to have your job.**"

He tells the story of the incident the next morning to his supervisor. The human resources director, who also supervises the security staff, holds a meeting to discuss the complaint. The guard's report says that he was carrying a computer down the hall and did not have a badge showing. The report also says that he used profanity.

He protests vigorously that the report is false, but it is his word against the guard's. The human resources director says: "*Well, it just looks like there's been a misunderstanding here, so we won't put anything in your file this time...*"

He realizes that the director's remarks are directed towards him.

"*...but come in through the security entrance, the next time you decide to come in after hours, and sign in the log. If something gets taken, we wouldn't want you to be a suspect.*"

"**This is outrageous. The guard has lied and now you treat me like I did something wrong.**"

"*You're overreacting. Don't be so sensitive.*"

He needs the money, so he doesn't follow his inclination to quit then, but he decides that as soon as he gets that M.B.A., he's going to a another company.

This is the kind of gauntlet an African-American must pass through to become successful in this country. As this example

SUCCESS SECRETS OF BLACK EXECUTIVES

demonstrates, very few of us can make it without the active help of mentors who take an interest in us and bandage us up after the latest wound from racism.

As our interviews with top executives demonstrate, it usually gets worse the higher one advances along the corporate ladder. White ignorance of African-Americans is deep-seated and endemic and the more encounters one has, the greater the likelihood of Freudian slips, even in the bedroom.

Each incident of personal or institutional racism takes a toll on the individual and through them on the collective self-esteem of African-America. As one award-winning newspaper editor told a potential employer after scoring the highest score in the history of the newspaper's management test, but being told that he wouldn't get the job: "If I can't make it in America, why should the brother on the corner even try."

One of the biggest impacts is a tendency to settle for a level of comfort, to keep quiet, not make any waves, and focus on self-gratification, whether it be an extensive flower garden or partying every night.

To step forward opens one up to more rejection, more racism and more pain, without hope for an end to it.

That state, whether evidenced by the welfare mother content to receive AFDC checks or the corporate vice president waxing his Jaguar, is the biggest impediment to African-American progress in America.

We're afraid to face any more pain than we have to.

As long as we are, we're still slaves.

Slaves are content to have their survival needs taken care of in return for the security of knowing that they belong somewhere -- "in their place."

Free people understand the value of pain as a great motivator and teacher. They accept the torture of racism, lick their wounds and redouble their effort to overcome it.

The first and second stages of black business had that determination. Pioneers like Paul Cuffee, Jean Baptiste DuSable,

Success Secrets of Black Executives

William Leidesdorff or Pio Pico understood that their pain gave them an advantage. They were capable of overcoming situations that would break their competitors.

In the third stage, many share that determination, but some have achieved just enough success to make themselves comfortable, but not do much for the group as a whole. Those businesses will not survive the test of time.

Fourth stage businesses have to understand the nature of the beast. We have to work together to deal with the pain of racism. The first armor that we can have is a knowledge of our history. Nothing gets to the roots of one's self-esteem more than knowing the history of one's own family and peoples.

Before going into business, thoroughly research the history of blacks in your own community and in your industry. You'll be invigorated and also wisened. You'll see their accomplishments and you'll see the factors that tripped them up. With that determination and that wisdom, you'll be able to build on their successes.

Build a forward and a backward network. The forward network would consist of persons with more experience than you. The backward network would stretch down into grade schools with people that you influence. There will be times when you need to look up to someone and times when you need to be looked up to.

If you're really committed, invest several hours in sessions with a professional therapist to explore your own hidden barriers to success. Do this before you go into business, because those barriers will dog you at every level unless you identify and address them.

Most of us could never recognize the impact that racism has on our lives because of the level of self-denial we consider necessary to survive. We take out on each other the feelings we would like to express to others, but have been trained to suppress for fear of our lives, liberty and possessions.

American brutality, physical or intellectual, toward black self-expression has been unrelenting and unmerciful. During a Congressional debate on the death penalty in 1990, a shocking fact emerged: no white person in American history has ever been

From The Editors Of ASPIRE

executed for the death of a black person. Our lives went from having 3/5ths value in the original Constitution to having none in the Dred Scott decision of 1857. There's been a steady movement up since then, but there is still an awful long way to go.

Co-dependency means that we do not grow into the full emotional maturity, taking ownership of our own feelings, our own needs and our own desires.

The survival of American racism depends on our maintaining that state.

The survival of African-Americans depends on our overcoming it.

Fourth stage black businesses are the vanguard of the black liberation struggle for the 21st century.

Our political progress has meant very little without economic force behind it.

Racism has forced us to think small. However, freedom is the ability to let one's imagination soar freely like the birds of the sky.

By learning our history, taking an international perspective on the world, by preparing our mastery, indispensibility, risk-taking, creativity, determination and by working cooperatively, we can build the kind of enterprises that take care of our needs as people -- for jobs, homes, families, schools, churches, cultural institutions.

We'll find that racism will fade into the background, like any other bully. As long as we believe the bully can whip us, we're beaten. When we stand up and stand-up together, the bully is already defeated.

Hopefully, you'll unshackle your own chains and take a step for freedom by launching a fourth stage business.

Even if you don't make it the first time, you'll learn lessons that will keep you along the roadway to success.

Success Secrets of Black Executives

FROM THE EDITORS OF ASPIRE

APPENDIX I
Family Income of African-Americans

Source: Current Population Survey, U.S. Census Bureau, 1989

Family Type	Number	Median Income
All Families	7,470,000	$20.209
Non-Farm	7,453,000	$20,248
Farm	17,000	n/a
Inside Metropolitan Areas	6,256,000	$21,593
1,000,000 or more	4,416,000	$22,986
Inside Central City	2,949,000	$19,472
Outside Central City	1,467,000	$32,270
Under 1,000,000	1,839,000	$19,037
Inside Central City	1,248,000	$18,531
Outside Central City	591,000	$20,001
Outside Metropolitan Areas	1,215,000	$14,370
Regional		
Northeast	1,279,000	$25,391
Midwest	1,446,000	$18,301
South	4,147,000	$19,029
West	598,000	$25,670
Type of family		
Married Couple	3,750,000	$30,650
Wife in Labor Force	2,400,000	$37,787
Not in Labor Force	1,345,000	$18,727
Male Households	446,000	$18,395
Female Households	3,275,000	$11,630

FROM THE EDITORS OF ASPIRE

APPENDIX II
African-American Educational Attainment

Years Completed	Number	HSG%age	1-3	4+	Median Years Completed
Black Population					
Over 25	16,395,000	38.5	18.3	11.8	12.4
25-29	2,726,000	47.8	21.9	12.7	12.7
30-34	2,662,000	44.1	25	13.9	12.7
35-44	3,900,000	41.3	20.3	16.7	12.7
45-54	2,565,000	35.9	12.4	11.8	12.3
55-64	2,105,000	26.5	9.8	6.9	11.4
65 plus	2,436,000	15.8	4.1	4.5	8.5

APPENDIX III
Sources on Business Formation

How to Start and Succeed in Business: A Special Guide for Small, Minority and Women-Owned Businesses California Commission on Economic Development (To obtain, call (415) 557-2662 or (213) 412-6118)

A Guide to Business Credit for Women, Minorities and Small Businesses Publications Services, Board of Governors, Federal Reserve System, Washington, D.C. 20551

California Small Business Guide to Government Services Senate Select Committee on Small Business Enterprises. Joint Publications, State Capitol, Box 942849, Sacramento, CA 94249-0001

Measuring Minority Business Formation and Failure, by Richard Stevens, Office of Program Support, Minority Business Development Agency, U.S. Department of Commerce, Room 5073, Washington, D.C. 20230

New Perspectives on Minority Business Development: A Study of Minority Business Potential Using the MBDA Financial Research Data Base Timothy Bates and Antonio Furino Office of Program Support, Minority Business

FROM THE EDITORS OF

Development Agency, U.S. Department of Commerce, Room 5073, Washington, D.C. 20230

Report on New Initiatives, Techniques and Incentives for Increasing Subcontracting Opportunities for Small Disadvantaged Businesses Owen Birnbaum Small Business Administration, P.O. Box 15434, Fort Worth, TX

Can You Make Money With Your Idea or Invention Small Business Administration, P.O. Box 15434, Fort Worth, TX

Introduction to Patents Small Business Administration, P.O. Box 15434, Fort Worth, TX

Going Into Business Small Business Administration, P.O. Box 15434, Fort Worth, TX

Business Plan for Small Service Firms Small Business Administration, P.O. Box 15434, Fort Worth, TX

Business Plan for Retailers Small Business Administration, P.O. Box 15434, Fort Worth, TX

Business Plan for Small Manufacturers Small Business Administration, P.O. Box 15434, Fort Worth, TX

Planning and Goal Setting for Small Business Small Business Administration, P.O. Box 15434, Fort Worth, TX

Business Plan for Home-Based Businesses Small Business Administration, P.O. Box 15434, Fort Worth, TX

How to Buy or Sell a Business   Small Business Administration, P.O. Box 15434, Fort Worth, TX

Developing a Strategic Business Plan   Small Business Administration, P.O. Box 15434, Fort Worth, TX

Evaluating Franchise Opportunities   Small Business Administration, P.O. Box 15434, Fort Worth, TX

ABC's of Borrowing   Small Business Administration, P.O. Box 15434, Fort Worth, TX

Profit Costing and Pricing for Manufacturers   Small Business Administration, P.O. Box 15434, Fort Worth, TX

Basic Budgets for Profit Planning   Small Business Administration, P.O. Box 15434, Fort Worth, TX

Understanding Cash Flow   Small Business Administration, P.O. Box 15434, Fort Worth, TX

A Venture Capital Primer for Small Business   Small Business Administration, P.O. Box 15434, Fort Worth, TX

Breakeven Analysis: A Decision-Making Tool   Small Business Administration, P.O. Box 15434, Fort Worth, TX

Pricing Products and Services Profitably   Small Business Administration, P.O. Box 15434, Fort Worth, TX

Effective Business Communications   Small Business Administration, P.O. Box 15434, Fort Worth, TX

Small Business Risk Management Guide   Small Business

FROM THE EDITORS OF ASPIRE

Administration, P.O. Box 15434, Fort Worth, TX

<u>Creative Selling</u> Small Business Administration, P.O. Box 15434, Fort Worth, TX

<u>Marketing for Small Business</u> Small Business Administration, P.O. Box 15434, Fort Worth, TX

<u>Is the Independent Sales Agent for You</u> Small Business Administration, P.O. Box 15434, Fort Worth, TX

<u>Marketing Checklist for Small Retailers</u> Small Business Administration, P.O. Box 15434, Fort Worth, TX

<u>Research Your Market</u> Small Business Administration, P.O. Box 15434, Fort Worth, TX

<u>Selling by Mail Order</u> Small Business Administration, P.O. Box 15434, Fort Worth, TX

<u>Market Overseas with U.S. Government Help</u> Small Business Administration, P.O. Box 15434, Fort Worth, TX

<u>Advertising</u> Small Business Administration, P.O. Box 15434, Fort Worth, TX

<u>Inventory Management</u> Small Business Administration, P.O. Box 15434, Fort Worth, TX

<u>Purchasing for Owners of Small Plants</u> Small Business Administration, P.O. Box 15434, Fort Worth, TX

<u>Fixing Production Mistakes</u> Small Business

Administration, P.O. Box 15434, Fort Worth, TX

Video Tapes

Marketing: Winning Customers with a Workable Plan Small Business Administration, P.O. Box 15434, Fort Worth, TX

The Business Plan: Your Roadmap to Success Small Business Administration, P.O. Box 15434, Fort Worth, TX

Promotion: Solving the Puzzle Small Business Administration, P.O. Box 15434, Fort Worth, TX

CD-ROM

The National Trade Data Bank released monthly by the U.S. Department of Commerce Economics and Statistics Administration HCHB Room 4885 Washington, D.C. 20230 (202) 377-1986 contains 90,000 documents including basic export information, country-specific information, industry-specific information, and industry-country information. NTDB's Foreign Traders Index identifies foreign firms seeking to import U.S. products.

From the Editors of ASPIRE

APPENDIX IV
Other Resources

U.S. Department of Commerce

Minority Business Development Agency

Communications Division

14th & Constitution Avenue

Washington, D.C. 20230

(202) 377-1936

Operates Minority Business Development Centers in all 50 states. Contact for the list, updated each month.

Office of Procurement Assistance

U.S. Small Business Administration

1441 L St. N.W.

Washington, D.C. 20416

(202) 653-6635

Operates 10 Regional Procurement and Technical Assistance Offices to provide assistance with federal contracting and government programs.

Export-Import Bank

811 Vermont Ave. N.W.

Washington, D.C.

(800) 424-5201

Overseas Private Investment Corp.

1615 M St. N.W.

Washington, D.C. 20527

(800) 424-6742

U.S. Trade and Development Program

International Development Cooperation Agency

U.S. Department of State

SA-16, Rm. 309

Washington, D.C. 20523-1602

(703) 875-4357

This program funds feasibility studies, consultancies, training programs and project planning for development projects in developing countries with large export potential, positioning U.S. firms for follow-on contracts. Examples include airports, railways, roads, schools, energy and data communications.

Foreign Agricultural Service

14th & Independence Ave. S.W.

Washington, D.C. 20520

(202) 447-7115

Most states also have:

Offices of Small and Minority Business

World Trade Commissions

The Small Business Administration also operates at the local levels:

Small Business Institutes at public and private universities

Small Business Development Centers at community colleges

Women's Network for Entrepreneural Training

Service Corps of Retired Executives

Active Corps of Executives

Contact your district office for more information on these programs.

FROM THE EDITORS OF

APPENDIX V
Procurement

The General Services Administration operates 12 Business Service Centers which are the front door to doing business with the U.S. government. Their addresses are:

Region 1

(CT, ME, MA, NH, RI, VT)

10 Causeway St.

Boston, MA 02222

(617) 565-8100

Region 2

(NY, NJ, PR, VI)

26 Federal Plaza

New York, NY 10278

(212) 264-1234

National Capitol Region

(DC, MD-VA Metro Area)

7th & D Sts. SW, Rm 1050

Washington, D.C. 20407

(202) 708-5804

Region 3

(PA, DE, MD, VA, WV)

9th & Market Sts., Rm. 5151

Philadelphia, PA 19107

(215) 597-9613

Region 4

(NC, SC, TN, MS, AL, GA, FL, KY)

75 Spring St, SW

Atlanta, GA 30303

(404) 331-5103

Region 5

(IL, WI, MI, IN, OH, MN)

230 S. Dearborn St.

Chicago, IL 60604

(312) 353-5383

Region 6

(KS, IA, MO, NE)

1500 E. Bannister Rd.

FROM THE EDITORS OF

Kansas City, MO 64131

(816) 926-7203

Region 7

(AR, LA, NM, OK, TX)

819 Taylor St., Rm 6A04

Fort Worth, TX 76102

(817) 334-3284

Region 8

(CO, WY, MT, UT, ND, SD)

Denver Federal Center

Building 41

Denver, CO 80225

(303) 236-7408

Region 9

(No CA, HI, NV)

525 Market St.

San Francisco, CA 94105

(415) 744-5050

(AZ, So CA, Nevada)

300 N. Los Angeles St.

Los Angeles, CA 90012-2000

(213) 894-3210

Region 10

(WA, OR, ID, AK)

15&C Sts. NW

Auburn, WA 98001

(206) 931-7956

In addition, some commodities are handled through these centers:

General Services Administration

Information Resources

Management Services (RMS)

Washington, DC 20405

Group 58 - Communication, Detection, Coherent Radiation Equipment

Group 70 - General Purpose Automatic Data Processing

FROM THE EDITORS OF

Equipment, Hardware, Software, Supplies and Support Equipment

Defense Electronics Supply Center

1507 Wilmington Pike

Dayton, OH 45401

(513) 296-6161

Group 59 - Electrical and Electronic Equipment Components

Group 60 - Fiber Optics Materials, Components, Assemblies

Defense General Supply Center

Bellwood, Petersburg Pike

Richmond, VA 23297

(804) 275-3679

Group 59

Group 61 - Electric Wire and Power Distribution Equipment

Defense Fuel Supply Center

Cameron Station, Bldg. 8

5010 Duke St.

Alexandria, VA 22314

(703) 274-6489

Group 91 - Fuels, Lubricants, Oils and Waxes

Defense Construction Supply Center

3990 East Broad St.

Columbus, OH 43215

(614) 238-3541

Veterans Administration Marketing Center

P.O. Box 76

Hines, IL 60141

(312) 343-7200

Group 65-Medical, Dental and Veterinary Equipment & Supplies

Group 89 - Subsistence

FROM THE EDITORS OF ASPIRE

APPENDIX IV
African-American Contributions to American Industrial Development

Sources: Robert C. Hayden in Van Sertima, Ivan (ed.)
<u>Blacks in science: ancient and modern</u>
Portia P. James "<u>The Real McCoy: African-American inventors</u>
Vivian O.Sammons, <u>Blacks in Science & Medicine</u>
William Lee, Ph.d, <u>Black Business in California</u> special section, The Sacramento Observer

Selected 19th Century Patent Holders

Name	Invention	Date	Patent #
A.J. Beard	Car Coupler	11/23/1897	597,059
C.B. Brooks	Street Sweeper	3/17/1896	556,711
J.D. Burr	Lawn Mower	5/09/1899	624,749
R.A. Butler	Train Alarm	6/15/1899	584,540
W.S. Campbell	Animal Trap	8/30/1881	246,369
F.J. Farrell	Steam Engine Valves	5/27/1890	428,671
G.T. Grant	Golf Tee	12/12/1899	638,920
M. Headen	Foot powered hammer	10/05/1886	350,363
J. Lee	Bread crumbing mach.	6/04/1895	540,553
J. Matzeliger	Shoe lasting mach.	9/22/1891	459,899
Elijah McCoy	Steam engine lubric.	7/02/1872	129,843
G.W. Murray	Fertilizer distributor	6/05/1894	520,889
W.P. Purvis	Paper bag machine	1/28/1890	420,099
G.T. Sampson	Clothes drier	6/07/1892	476,416
J.P. Winters	Fire escape ladder	5/07/1878	203,517

Early 20th Century Industrial Enterprises and Impact

<u>Elijah McCoy Manufacturing Co., Detroit</u> Invented railroad lubrication process that dominated the market and was the source of the term "the real McCoy" because his product was regarded as the highest quality device.

<u>Woods Electrical Co., Cincinnati, Ohio</u> won a patent battle with Thomas Edison over telegraph system. Granville T. Woods' 35 patents included improvements to telephones, electric lights and telegraphy to reach a moving train. Many of his innovations contributed to the development of the electric street car including his invention of th e "troller" wheel, which grew into the name of "trolley" to describe the street cars Sold patents to American Bell Telephone, General Electric and Westinghouse Air Brake

<u>Parker Machine and Foundry Co.</u> Invented tobacco screw press that dramatically improved manufacturing processes

<u>C.R. Patterson & Co. Greenfield, Ohio</u> built the Patterson-Greenfield family car beginning in 1916 for $850 and custom bodies for ice, milk, furniture, bakery and other specialized trucks as well as buses and hearses. Also built the buses for Cincinnati's transit system Company survived until 1938.

<u>ThermoKing Corp.</u> Frederick McKinley Jones received 60 patents, including 40 for refrigeration systems. He created the first practical truck refrigeration system, portable X-ray machines, movie sound equipment, a self-starting gasoline engine, a reverse cycling mechanism for producing heat and cold, and air temperature and moisture controls.

FROM THE EDITORS OF ASPIRE

Selected 20th Century Scientific and Technical Innovators

<u>Lewis Latimer</u> -- made the first drawings of Alexander Graham Bell's telephone and then began own career as an inventor and patent expert. He invented the first long-lasting carbon filaments for the electric light bulb, making Edison's invention a practical consumer product, and wrote the first textbook on incandescent electric lighting. He supervised the installation of electric lights in New York, Philadelphia and London.

<u>Elmer S. Jones</u> -- his 1919 doctoral dissertation established that quantum theory could be extended to include the rotational states of molecules.

<u>Dr. Lloyd Quarterman</u> and six other black scientists played key roles in the Manhattan Project which created the atomic bomb that ended World War II.

For a more expanded listing of the contributions of black scientists and researchers, refer to:

Vivian C. Sammons, <u>Blacks in Science and Medicine</u> lists 1,500 scientists including backgrounds, specialities and significant accomplishments

Hattie Carwell, <u>Blacks in Science: Astrophysicist to Zoologist</u>

FROM THE EDITORS OF ASPIRE